NEW VISION
PUBLICATION
PRESENTS

Thicker Than BLOOD

A NOVEL BY
KAMERON D.

This novel is a work of fiction. Any references to real people, events, establishments, or locales are intended only to give the fiction a sense of reality and authenticity. Other names, characters, and incidents occurring in the work are either the product of the author's imagination or are used fictitiously, as those fictionalized events and incidents that involve real persons. Any character that happens to share the name of a person who is an acquaintance of the author, past or present, is purely coincidental and is in no way intended to be an actual account involving that person.

ISBN: (13) 978-0-9836039-3-1
Cover design: www.mariondesigns.com
Inside layout: www.mariondesigns.com
Editors: Jazzy Editorial Services

Thicker Than blood/Kameron D.

NEW VISION
P.O. Box 2815
Stockbridge, GA 30281
www.newvisionpublication.com

First Printing December 2011
Printed in U.S.A.

10   9   8   7   6   5   4   3   2   1

Dedication

This book is dedicated to all of those that believed
and supported me through it all.

New Vision
PUBLICATION
PRESENTS

Thicker Than BLOOD

There's no stronger bond than family...Especially when someone is trying to take you out!

A NOVEL BY
KAMERON D.

Prologue

Total-E heard the intruders stumbling around on the first floor. He knew exactly where they were, because he could distinctly hear the sounds of the broken glass he scattered among the debris breaking as they moved around. Stepping into the janitor's closet that he'd been standing in front of, he brought up the smooth barrel of a Remington pump shotgun. Jerking it upwards, in a much practiced move, he caught the pistol grip and slipped a finger inside the trigger guard.

Pulling the door quietly closed, he squatted and focused on the hole in the door made by a sixteen-penny nail. Though his field of vision was narrowed, he could still see the steps and the top landing above them.

It took thirty-two seconds longer than he'd estimated for the two men to reach the third floor. Through the hole, he watched them bring their heads together as they whispered and drew their weapons from beneath their jackets.

Eyes upwards towards the fourth floor, the two men moved quietly on their toes, guns ready.

"*Stupid niggas!*" Total thought angrily. This was supposed to be a simple meet, to both pay him the remainder of his fee and advance him the first half of the money for the next job. Instead, they'd showed up an hour early with guns in their hands, which could mean only one thing. Trench was crossing him and crosses of any sort were unacceptable.

Pushing the door open with the tips of his fingers, Total extended the shotgun and pulled the trigger. As the shotgun bucked, he caught the pump with his left hand and jacked in a second round even before he saw the damage the first one had done.

"Behind us move!" the lead man screamed and took the stairs two, three and four at a time.

The warning had been senseless, because his partner was rolling back down the stairs a chunk of flesh from the base of his skull missing. He wasn't dead, but he would be before his partner landed four flights down in the abandoned buildings basement, after stepping onto the rug-covered hole at the top of the landing.

Tossing the shotgun, Total pulled the Heckler & Koch 9mm from his waistband. He stopped moving, just long enough to attach the silencer and fire two wasted rounds into the already dead man's head.

Spinning, he followed the screams to the basement.

Bently Jacobs was a mess--had always been a mess--where he lay twisted and impaled on several concrete reinforcement rods. One rod had gone through his back and protruded grossly from his stomach. Bently held onto, the bloody and rusted rod with both hands.

"Tell me what I need to hear," Total whispered, as he moved closer.

"Fuck you Total!" Bently groaned, as blood ran from between his lips and down his chin.

"No, fuck your wife and kids," Total replied not raising his voice, or showing any anxiety.

"You wouldn't...naw man," Bently said twisting his head so he could see Total's face. There was no salvation there.

"Your choice."

"Gimme your word...swear on it," Bently said grim-acing with pain.

"On everything I love!"

"Trench...Trench sent us. My wife...my babies?"

"They live." Total raised the gun to within an inch of Bently's temple and squeezed the trigger twice.

Chapter 1

Total E was in the day room playing cards when he heard the correctional officer call his name and institutional number, "B-1376 come report to the bridge immediately!" At first Total E acted like he didn't hear it and kept playing cards.

"Yo E, they calling you!"

"Nigga I ain't going nowhere until I'm done whipping your ass in this card game."

"B-1376 report to the bridge, now!"

Total E took his sweet time reaching the bridge. When he got there, the guard had a sad ass face. "You got to report to the chapel." Every body knows that when they call you to the chapel in prison, is not to pray. Total E knew that it wasn't good news. Once he reached the chapel the Reverend informed him that his father had died. He was allowed to make one free call from the Chaplain office, and he decided to call the only person he could depend on, Snow.

Ring! Ring! Ring! Snow phone vibrated in her bag. She didn't recognize the number, but only one person in the world had her number, so she answered it.

"Speak!" Snow said.

"It me, Total! I'm just calling because my father just pass away. I need you to arrange the funeral."

"Baby, consider it done! Do you want to attend?"

"Yes!" Snow was shock when Total answer yes, considering the way his father had disowned him, due to his life style, money, drugs and bitches.

"Baby, I'll be up there tomorrow to visit," Snow said. After they hung up, Total E made his way back to his housing unit. He locked himself in his cell, laying in bed plotting on how he was gonna get made revenge on all those pussy ass niggas who set him up. *Niggas are going to feel my pain. Nigga are gonna die! Niggas in Harlem will forever remember my name.* He thought to himself as he counted backwards the years he's been on lock down due to some sucka ass nigga. *Nine! Eight! Seven! Six! Five! Four! Three! Two! One! Nine fucking years! I can't believe this shit.*

❧

The follow day he received a visit from Snow and his old head Blaze. He was the first inmate out in the visiting room, which meant that Blaze must've pull some strings and flew out there instead of driving.

The minute Snow saw him, she teared up. "Damn baby, I'm sorry to hear about your father!" Snow said, giving him a hug.

"Total E, you grown up on me!" Blaze said, giving him a tight hug.

"Listen Snow! Give me a few minutes in private to talk with Blaze."

"I'll be over by the vending machine." While Snow was at the vending machine, Total E informed Blaze that his way out of prison was through his father funeral.

"It's either that or die in here!"

"Total, I love the idea, and I would help! I will make things happen in due time." Blaze changed the conversation when Snow returned to her seat.

"I already made the arrangement for the funeral, and paid for the sheriffs office to come pick you up and take you to the funeral. Everything is set for Monday morning. They only going to keep you there for two hours."

"Thank you baby! I knew I could count on you." Total E said, cracking a smirk at Blaze.

Once the visit was over, Total E went back to his cell and looked at the place he called home for the last nine years and wondered if the prisons walls were enough to keep him from touching a few well deserved niggas.

Chapter 2

Monday morning arrived fast, and a correctional officer opened Total E cell and called, "B-1376 wake the fuck up!" Total E faked as if he was asleep.

"What man?"

"Get up! Prepare for an escorted transportation. You have a funeral to attend!"

You should be lucky it's not your funeral asshole! Total E thought to himself as he stared at the guard.

He took a bird shower in his cell sink, and looked himself in the mirror and thought, *if my mother recognize me I would let my beard grow, and I would grow dreads.* Once he was done, he walked down to the guards office and informed the guard on duty that he was ready.

"What took you so long? Y'all niggas always want to get pretty! You only going to a funeral, and right back here, buddy! Now you got to wait for the intake officer to come and get you."

Total E just smiled at the guard. He wasn't bout to let him upset hm.

"I got no problem waiting! I been waiting nine hard years for this day." The guards just shook his head, and closed his eyes, trying to regain his sleep. It took the intake guard almost an hour to come get Total E. Once he was in the holding tank he sat and waited another hour, before he was giving some clothes that looked like something from the 70's. Afterward, two sheriffs handcuffed and shackle him up, then escorted him onto a mini van with a big Department of Correction logo on it.

On the way to Harlem the sheriffs made a stop for some food and offered Total E something to eat. It had been nine years since Total E had any street food, but he turned their offer down.

Once they reach the sign Welcome to Harlem, Total E was energized. He instantly remembered the times when he was king of the area.

Once in front of the funeral home, one of the sheriffs got out the van and entered the funeral home to make sure everything was clear. Then he came back outside and took Total E out the van and into the funeral home.

"I would take off the handcuffs, but not the shackles," one of the sheriffs said, removing the handcuffs. Once inside the room where his father casket sat, he walked to the casket and kneeled down. Suddenly, a familiar voice asked him, "Sir are you alright?" Total E looked up, and to his surprise it was Blaze. Total E smiled, and faked a tear as Blaze handed him a tissue with a note in it, then walked away toward the two sheriffs, handing them a bottle of water each. They both tilt their head up to drink the water, when they saw the casket with Total E father and Total E kneeling down being lowered toward the basement. But, before they could react, Blaze already had his gun aiming at their head. They both dropped to the floor in slow motion.

Total E was already in a crown vic with tinted windows enjoying his first day of freedom. The driver of the car, handed Total E a cell phone when it rang.

"Welcome back to the block!" Blaze said as Total E inquired about Snow.

"Where is Snow?"

"Total E! My job was to get you home!" Blaze responded, hanging up the phone. Total dialed Snow number and instructed her to meet him where he used to sleep as a young boy. The driver of the car dropped Total E off at Central Park. Total E couldn't wait to see Snow.

Chapter 3

Aljiva Snow waited until just seconds before the C-Train's doors were closing to step out and onto the platform. There was nobody on the platform towards the front of the train. Exiting through the turnstile at the back was a couple holding hands as they squeezed through it pressed together and giggling. Hefting her leather and canvas knapsack, Snow, headed towards the front of the train platform and the 109th Street exit, and she wasn't diverting from them.

Going out the rear exit, would have placed Snow within a block of her destination--Morningside Park--but the instructions had specifically said for her to use the front exit out onto 109th.

Coming out of the subway, Snow trembled slightly as the cold breeze that whipped around her. Central Park with piles of dirty snow was to her right. To her left, were more mounds of snow and Manhattan Avenue. The block leading to Manhattan Avenue was poorly lit, but she had her instructions. Stepping off the curb, Snow crossed the street, but decided to walk out in it, the light there made her feel a whole lot more comfortable.

Halfway along the block, Snow spied a bundled-up, stooped figure going through a pile of blue recycling bags and tossing the cans into a wheeled canvas cart. Just after she passed him, a huge New York rat trying to pull half a Thanksgiving Day turkey from a black garbage bag, lost its grip and flipped backwards.

"Oh fucking no!" Snow cried out aloud and danced backwards and sideways into the path of an oncoming SUV.

"Drunken bitch! Get the fuck out the way," the SUV's driver screamed out the open window and shot up a finger, as he swerved to keep from hitting her.

Snow's mittened hand came from her hooded goose jacket, as she pulled out a small but deadly two-shot .38.

"I got your drunken bitch!" Snow screamed in both anger and fear, but her eyes never leaving the area where the rat had darted back into the pile of bags.

"Get to the park and stop that fucking cussing!" the bent over figure near the blue bags barked.

"Jasper...."

"Jasper shit! Put that shit back in your pocket and go...I got you," the man said cutting Snow off.

Snow wasn't used to having people tell her what to, or not to do, but this time she obeyed. At Manhattan Avenue she made a right and before she knew it, she was skipping down the wide, freshly salted steps into Morningside Park.

The park seemed dead at two in the morning, but Snow knew better. The park was a haven for crackheads looking for dead-like spots to smoke without being interrupted. She moved through the dusky darkness, but not as careful as she would have if she had not heard those three words. *"I got you."*

Midway through the park between 113th and 114th, she headed left and went up the stairs. Halfway up the stairs, she spotted the broken forty-ounce bottle and stepped off the stairs. There was a barely discernable path leading between some stunted spruce trees and prickly bushes. She stopped when she came to the point where she'd have to go down a snow-covered hill. Turning to go back the way she'd come, she came face to face with one of the most wanted men in New York state.

"Look at you," Total said shaking his head slowly. "One of the most beautiful women in the City and you're thugged out like some dude in baggy jeans and Timbs.

Before Snow could think of a response, Total reached out using both hands to swipe the hood of her coat back. He stared deep into her eyes for a half a beat, then stepped closer and pressed his lips to hers.

He had forgotten just how soft and supple Snow's full lips were.

Snow parted her lips and allowed Total's tongue into her mouth. A tingling sensation began somewhere in the pit of her stomach. She suckled on his tongue for several seconds, and then fed him hers.

"I'm not a dyke...not one," Snow muttered, partially breaking the kiss.

"I know...know and understand," Total replied, then kissed the woman that had intruded every dream he'd had for the past nine years, hard and hungrily. The ground under him, felt like it shifted and his dick jerked and began growing hard. *Damn! I got to get my dick wet!*

Feeling Total's hardness, Snow pressed her body even tighter against his. They both gasped and sucked for air as their hands explored each other's bodies.

"Not like this," Total whispered as he nuzzled Snow's perfumed ear, realizing that she was trying to get his jeans unfastened. Snow persisted and he had to take both of her mitten hands in his to stop her.

"Let me suck your dick right now." Snow said.

"Nah! It had been nine years, two months and five days since I last touched you. My hunger for you is great, if not greater than your own, but the park isn't the place for what I wanted...needed. So let's just wait. Trust me, we gonna fuck." He gave her a consolation peek on her lips, then added, "Forty minutes won't kill us," staring into her teared and

13

glistening brown eyes. "Trust me," he pleaded, taking the hood of her jacket and lifting it back up over her short, waved head.

Taking Snow's hand, Total lead her back out and onto the steps. They continued on up the stairs towards Broadway, where the One-Train waited for them.

"Always have," Snow whispered in a delayed response as she hooked her arm beneath Total's and leaned her head against his broad shoulders.

Chapter 4

The intense heat that had begun building in Morningside Park grew and grew and by the time they reached the Terminal Hotel on 23rd and 11th Avenue, it had all but consumed them.

Total entered the room first and turned to set aside the knapsack he'd taken from Snow. He turned at the sound of the door being slammed closed and Snow was all over him. As they kissed and stroked each other's bodies, their clothes came off. Naked, Total hesitated just long enough to engrave the image of Snow naked body onto his brain, then scooped her up and carried her over to the bed.

"Please...please?" Snow panted, as Total licked and sucked on her blackberry-colored nipples, causing them to grow even harder and thicker. She tried to stop him, when he began licking and kissing his way down the soft downy line of hair that covered her flat stomach. But, as always it was Total's way or no way.

"Arrrrrghhh! Shit!" Snow screamed, as Total ran his tongue straight up the crack of her ass and through her hairless cunt-lips. When he drove his tongue into her, she grabbed the extra pillow and bunched it against her face. Screaming into the pillow, Snow shivered and shook like her body was coming apart.

"I been waiting nine years to do this baby," Total said, as he moved his dick between her legs. Snow pussy was already wet, and he kept it wet by massaging it with his hot dick. He reached up and caressed her blackberry-colored nipples as he continued to play with her pussy. He drew some of her pussy juice back to the bottom of her asshole.

Snow tensed instinctively, and he pulled back.

"Damn! What the fuck were you doing in there! All of a sudden you want some ass." Snow said, not knowing if she could take it in the ass.

"Easy baby, it hurts if you're tight. Just relax and it'll slide right in. It's wet enough."

Snow never imagined submitting to no back door action, but she loved Total so much she was willing to let him have his way. Her body relaxed.

Then she felt the full penetration of his dick head. It seemed to grow, to generate heat inside of her.

"Shake that ass for me, baby."

Snow began to rotate, her ass, hoping Total would come fast, but instead he began to go deeper into her. She tried to squeeze his dick, but he pulled back. Snow resigned herself to let Total have his piece of ass.

16

She wiggled and squirmed, her fucking body was on fire, as Total dick moved in and out of her asshole.

"Push that ass back!"

Snow knew Total was about to bust his guns. She almost fainted from the pain and pleasure as he fucked into her fat ass with major force.

"I'm gonna drop my babies in your ass now. Snow. Ooooo, yessss, baby keep it tight for meeeee."

"Come on nigga give that good dick. Ooooooo." Snow let out in a poetic burst.

Total was in another world, his hunger for ass was severe. As his balls tighten, he pushed deep, his thick dick entered Snow's ass completely.

Snow's ass cheeks wriggled under his force. His hot cum shot into her, warming her asshole. Snow gasped for breath.

"Total, that was good," Snow said.

❧

Turning Snow's arm over as she slept, Total checked the time. It was just after four in the morning. Getting out of bed, Total used one of the towels from the nightstand to dry the remaining sweat from his hard muscular body. The towel slung around his neck, he went to the piles of clothes near the door. Searching the pockets of Snow's jacket, he pulled out first the derringer and then her cell phone. Putting the gun back, he picked up the knapsack and carried it over to a small faded loveseat.

The first thing Total found in the knapsack was his old .44 caliber Desert Eagle. Rummaging deeper, he found what he was really looking for, a Smith and Wesson 9mm with a perforated silencer attached. After checking to be sure the gun was loaded, he set it aside and dug for the shoulder-holster. He found it at the bottom of the bag. Slipping into the harness, he removed the silencer from the gun and shoved it home. For the first time in a whole lot of years, he didn't feel naked, even though he was.

Taking a quick glance towards Snow's sleeping form, Total picked up the phone and flipped it open. He hadn't seen one like it, but it looked easy enough to operate. From memory, he dialed number and listened to it ring twice, before someone answered.

"Gottcha T...been waiting," the wide-awoke voice said.

"How'd you know it was me?"

"You're the only one with this number."

Total chuckled. "Look, I need a babysitter.

"Blaze a babysitter?"

"Yeah man, for now," Total replied.

"Must be one....It ain't that baby everybody's been looking for, including me would it?"

"You got it. She's the most important baby in the world as far as I'm concerned."

"Then I'm a babysitter. How soon you need me to go to work?"

Total turned again and looked towards Snow's uncovered thigh and leg. Raising his eyes, he watched the rise and fall of her breast.

"You still there T?" Blaze questioned the silence.

"Nine's good for me," Total finally answered, feeling himself become yet again aroused.

"Where's the baby?"

"The End with me," Total answered, using the nickname they had for the Terminal Hotel. "Room 201," he added and pressed the red icon to end the call.

Turning to sit the phone down, Total found Snow starting to kneel beside him.

"Your turn," she offered simply in explanation and pried total's knees apart so she could position herself in between them.

Total slid forward on the loveseat from his waist down, knowing that resisting was futile. Taking the ends of the towel around his neck into his hands, he watched Snow kissing and licking him until he was completely hard. When she levered herself up, using his thighs for braces, he watched her open her mouth and then closed his eyes.

"I'm going to such your dick real good! Snow said. She could feel her jaw beginning to hurt as she tried to deep throat Total horse dick down. This was a crucial time.

In between suck's she would look at Total and said, "I love the way your dick taste."

Total was lost in a world of lust.

Chapter 5

With the arrival of Blaze, both Snow and Total had reverted back to the days when he'd taken them to Coney Island or even into Jersey to Great Adventure. At the sight of Blaze's awesome 6'6," 390 pounds and his still youthful appearance, Snow had run to him and jumped up into his arms. Blaze caught her and kissed her like a long, lost child.

Blaze was sixty, if he had been both Snow's father's mentor and one time partner. To Snow, he was Granddad, to Total he was Uncle Blaze. It had been at least two years before Total had gone to prison, when they had last seen him. It had been rumored, that he'd gone back to North Carolina and quietly died.

When Total had told her she was going to have a babysitter, she'd gone ballistic---swearing as usual---and claimed her right to stand next to him, with whatever happened. Total's assured her that when it was time to put in work that she'd be with him, she backed down and agreed to stay put with Blaze.

Blaze had come prepared for any eventualities. Not only had he come with a forty-eight quart ice chest filled with food and drink, but he brought three Second-Chance Kevlar vest and a baby suitcase full of weapons. The three of them had shared a breakfast of turkey and swiss on rye with orange juice. Afterwards, Total had put on one of the vest beneath his derelict outfit and left after kissing Snow and getting the keys to Blaze's car.

Blaze had moved the television so he could see it and watch the door to the room at the same time. Still tired from the early morning sucking and workout, she crawled back into bed. No sooner that her head hit the pillow, she was asleep and dreaming once again of the events that had lead up to the note being slipped under the door of the apartment in the Saint Nick projects.

Snow ordinarily didn't ride with her brothers Alex and Drew to make the money pickups from their lucrative drug business, but something had gone wrong with the electrical system of her Benz.. the steering wheel had locked and nothing she or her brothers had tried could get it unlocked. A tow truck from Triple-A had come for the car. With a choice between taking the subway back down to Midtown where she rested her head and having her brothers drive her home after they picked her up, she'd jumped into the backseat of Drew's Lexus.

The first five pickups had been both tedious and boring, with Snow playing the backseat, even when they went in to pick up the money. With the heat on high, to ward off the freezing cold from outside the car, Snow found herself dozing. She was dead asleep when they made the sixth stop and didn't know what was going on, until the front passenger window of the Lexus exploded and showered her with tiny fragments of glass.

Acting strictly on instincts, Snow dug into her shoulder bag and pulled free the .380 semi-automatic she carried. Lowering the rear passenger side window, as she raised her head, she saw and heard the flash and the booms of a big gun barking from inside the semi-dark hallway. Alex seemed to be snatched backwards out the doorway, landing with a fucked up sound thud. Drew came running out the building and had to hurdle the steps and Alex's sprawled form. As he hit the ground, he spun and began pumping rounds back through the doorway.

"Snow! Get the fuck out of here!" Drew screamed, as he snatched a peek towards the car and saw her.

Snow had been trained almost from birth to follow orders, but even as she scrambled over the seat into the front of the car, she squeezed off a half-dozen rounds at a shadow in the hallway.

Ducking below step-level, Drew moved sideways to check Alex, who still hadn't moved. "Shit!" he groaned and pulled the 9mm free from his brother's waistband. Raising up, he fired both weapons until they jammed back empty and then ran to the car.

"Go! Alex is dead!" he ordered jumping into the car.

Seeing movement near the front of the doorway, Snow extended her arm out across her brother's body and fired her last three rounds, even as she spun the steering wheel and stomped on the gas.

The car lurched forwarded swiveling and then straightened as it streaked down 153rd Street. A fusillade of heavy gunfire raked the rear of the car, shattering the back window.

At Riverside Drive, Snow made a screeching right. Drew slammed into her and stayed there even after she got the car straightened out. Using her right hand, she shoved him away from her. Her hand came away bloodied. Panic almost set in, but realizing that both of their lives depended on her maintaining control, she ignored the blood and took the wheel with both hands and drove.

It took several minutes and a series of wild turns, before Snow found the Westside Highway. She drove until she spotted the turnoff to Saint Luke's hospital.

Throwing open her door, she dug beneath the seat and found the bulging money bag. Snatching it, she ran through the automatic emergency room doors.

screaming. It took several precious seconds for Snow to make the security guard and the nurses understand that it wasn't her who was injured.

As a doctor, nurses and the security guard ran outside to the car, Snow walked quickly to the side exit door and stepped back out onto the streets. Making sure she stayed in the shadows, Snow waited until a cab approached and waved it down. When the driver got a look at her---when the interior light came on--he screamed for her to get out.

Digging into her own bag, Snow gathered up all the loose money she could find and dropped it over and onto the driver's seat. It had to be at least eight-hundred dollars there, so when she told the driver to drive, he drove.

On 30th Street, Snow had the cabbie drop her a couple doors from the lit sign that announced the place was a women's shelter. She moved towards it as the cab pulled off, but then dipped out the doorway as soon as it made a right on 7th Avenue. Hurrying up the dark block, she entered the rear entrance to the Meyer's parking lot. Foregoing the walk to the front where there was an elevator, she climbed the interior stairs to the third floor and found her Audi where she'd parked it that morning.

The Audi was her Downtown car. She'd never driven it above 59th and Columbus Circle. Had the Benz not been fucked up, she'd have driven it to the lot and switched over before heading to her crib in

Chelsea.

One pass through 13th Street, was enough to convince Snow that it wasn't a good idea to go home. Parked halfway down the block, was a white-on-white Denali that she and anybody from Harlem would recognize on sight. The truck belonged to Ting-a-ling and she thanked God, for having spent the extra money to tint the Audi's windows. As she drove by she saw Ting-a-ling and two other figures huddled in the doorway two doors from her place.

With so much going on in her head, Snow hadn't even realized that the building where they had killed Alex and maybe Drew was one that Ting-a-ling and his brother ran drugs from. The two of the brothers together didn't have enough heart or brains to pull off the jacking, but with a father like Ace Lake, it made one hell of a difference.

For almost three hours, Snow drove around senselessly. It was obvious from Ting-a-ling's presence at her house, that somebody had opened their mouth. Someone that was close to her, which meant it wasn't safe, nor wise to go anywhere she normally went. Parking the car on a dark side street, Snow thought. Twenty minutes later, she restarted the engine and pulled off with a purpose for the first time in hours.

At 4:37 in the morning, Snow cut her car lights and eased into a parking lot between 127th and 128th Streets. Finding an empty spot, she killed the engine and sat for a few moments in the dark, looking around at the buildings of the St. Nicholas projects, a place she used to call home.

Climbing quickly from the car and using the remote to set the alarm, she moved into the shadowy parts of the complex and made her way to the rear entrance of one of the buildings. Not wanting to meet anyone, that might recognize her, she took the back steps up to the fifth floor. Keys in hand, she rushed to the door, opened it and slipped inside throwing all three deadbolts behind her.

It had been more than five years since: anyone had actually lived in what had been her family's apartment and it both looked and smelled like it. Even in the dark, it felt safe and at that moment, safety was the most important thing in the world. She cried.

For the first three days, she'd made and gotten calls, but they all seemed to end the same way. With whomever she was speaking to wanting to know where she was. Though they didn't realize it, there was always emphasis on *"Where are you?"* and she wasn't feeling it one bit. She did however learn, that Drew was dead and that at least five members of her brothers' crew had been killed or shot to pieces. Her brothers' inner circle it seemed had vanished into thin air. Their phone numbers didn't even ring.

On the fourth day, necessity pushed Snow into the bathtub first and then into some of her really old clothes that had been left behind when they moved. Waiting until almost four in the morning, she snuck out of the building the same way she'd entered and made the drive to Jersey. Finding an all-night Wendy's with a drive-thru window, she ordered enough food to feed four people. She ate until she passed out and was woken by the sun shining through her side window.

There was no way she was going to risk trying to get back into her old building in the daytime, so she drove the highways and shopped.

Another two and a half weeks passed, with her leaving only to buy food and to keep the walls of the apartment from closing in on her. She'd just returned from one of her outings, when a knock came behind her on the door. It wasn't loud, but it had happened when it shouldn't have. As she stared terrified out of her mind, she saw the envelope as it was shoved beneath the door. For twenty minutes she stood unmoving, her eyes locked on the envelope. It took everything she had to go to it and finally pick it up.

Carrying the envelope to the couch where she'd been sleeping, she slowly tore it open. As soon as she unfolded the single sheet of lined paper, she recognized the handwriting. It was Jasper's... Total's... "*But how?*" her mind demanded. It was him; there was no mistaking his neat print, having gotten at least two letters a week from him for the past nine plus years. Laying the letter on the arm of the couch she read it slowly.

Dear Snow:

    As you read this letter you probably wondering if this is a joke! No, it's not. Don't worry how I located you; just know that I'm with you all the time. For nine years you been my rock and soul, now it's time for me to show you my love. I'll see you soon, sooner than you think.

Total

Chapter 6

Ten Years Later...

Total drove back and forth through Harlem and Washington Heights for two hours. Everybody that was anybody, knew him or had heard of him, but he seriously doubted that anyone not personally associated with him, would recognize him. It had been almost ten years since he'd been out in the world and the pictures they'd been showing on the news stations, showed him when he had first gotten arrested and had been on trial. He'd been the same 6'3," but he'd only weighed 157 pounds...his hair had been cut short and faded Jersey style...his face had been baby smooth, with nothing on it that even resembled hair. Now he was 227 pounds, his dreadlocks hung just below his pull-up-bar broadened shoulders and back and he wore a full beard.

What he was doing, was checking out Trench's old hustling spots. A lot of stuff in the world had changed, but most of Trench's spots seemed to still be in place. Trench wasn't the primary target, but he was a target. Ace Lake had been around since before Snow's father got slumped, but he'd never seemed to want anymore on his plate than what he already had. His sons were a new entity, one that he'd have to talk to Snow about a little more.

From what he gathered and been told by at least two of the three people that he felt safe talking to, Ace Lake and his boys were behind the deaths of Snow's brothers and possibly her father. What was weird though, was the timing. Total's last shot at getting his two life sentences overturned, had just been sandblasted two weeks before Alex and Drew had been slumped. The denial of his appeal meant, that he should have been doomed to spend a minimum of fifty years behind bars before he'd see the Parole Board the first time. They knew he was not just her muscle, but that he was without doubt the only man she'd ever had.

If he had been in Ace Lake's shoes, he too would have waited until he was positive he wouldn't have to deal with him. He'd dropped a lot of bodies in Snow's name, but not a single one had, or could ever be traced back to her. The years he was away were just barely enough time for Ace's sons to grow up and become the thugs they professed to be. If his thinking was on track, it was probably the sons' idea to remove Snow and her family. It wasn't that the sons didn't want more on their plates, they wanted the bigger plate.

Coincidence in timing or not, they'd killed Snow's brothers and had tried to get at her. They'd tried, failed and now had money out on her, taking him being in prison as a gimme. The way he had it figured, they wanted to play at murder when he'd never had an opportunity to "play." What Total knew and understood about murder came from putting in the work. Up close and personal.

❦

Even at just thirteen, Jasper Jefferies had seen the bullshit coming from the roof of the building he'd lived his whole life in. Aljiva Snow was slowly strolling up Fredrick Douglas, toward 127th Street. Across the street, Noonie and her brothers stood just around the corner and across from the St. Nick projects waiting. From time to time, one of the two brothers would peek around the corner. They became real animated at the sight of Snow.

Opening his too big goose down coat, Jasper clamped a hand around the broken kitchen knife he'd taken from Aljiva's house. The knife had spoken to him. *"They're going to hurt Snow for putting her foot in Noonie's fat ass behind you!"*

Pulling the knife out, Jasper spun away from the edge of the roof and ran to the exit door. Stepping through the door and into the building, he jumped across his sleeping bag and halfway down the stairs. Snatching open the door on the next level, he ran to the elevator kicking the beer can he'd put there inside, he jumped in and punched the lobby button.

In the lobby, Jasper forced himself not to run, as he worked the knife handle-first up into his sleeve. There was no sense in drawing unnecessary attention to himself.

At the corner, he watched Snow stop three-quarters of the way up the block to unscrew the top of a fifty-cent soda. Jasper knew it would be lemon-lime, even though he was to far away to see it. Lemon-lime was their shared favorite.

Glancing to his right, Jasper watched Noonie and her brothers leave the wall of the building where they had been standing and begin to cross the street at an angle, ignoring the oncoming traffic. Crossing 127th, Jasper sped up wanting to get there when they did, but staying in the street and using the line of parked cars to conceal him.

Noonie suddenly finding heart she hadn't had two days before, came from between two cars and shoved Aljiva from the side with both hands. Surprised, Snow dropped the soda and skipped back trying to keep the soda's spray from hitting her Timberlands.

"Now what bitch?" Noonie screamed, shoving Snow yet again.

"Fuck you...you and your brothers!" Aljiva shouted, dropping her book bag and turning to face the trio.

"Naw bitch, fuck you and your black assed Africa momma!" Roland, the oldest of the crew spit back and used his thigh to pop open the silver box cutter he held.

"Do him!" the knife hissed urgently, as Jasper let it slide from his sleeve down into his sweaty hand.

The next forty-two seconds were a blur--at least to Jasper's mind--but it all ended with Noonie's youngest brother Rayford, running out into the street screaming for somebody...anybody to call the police and an ambulance, as he ducked between and around moving and parked cars with Jasper chasing him.

Roland at seventeen caught the worse break of his Bodying young life. Jasper had swung the knife from his hip, intending to sink the blade into Roland's shoulder, but the shoulder wasn't there. Had Roland not raised his arm to slash downwards into Snow's face, it would have been there. Instead, the point and four inches of the chipped blade nestled itself into the soft, warm flesh of his armpit. He'd screamed like a scalded cat and bled out, long before the first police car or ambulance arrived on the scene. Noonie hadn't been so lucky either, but she was a lot luckier than her brother. It took a buck and change in stitches to close up the knife slash that started at her left temple and ended at her jawbone...it took another twenty-nine stitches to put her almost severed tongue back together.

Snow had been stunned at the pure viciousness of the attack. She'd somehow shaken herself free of the vice-like grip, as the screams of fifteen year-old Rayford reached her brain. She'd just barely kept Jasper from doing Rayford, by stepping into his line of vision and screaming, *"It's Snow!"*

When the first police car arrived, because of all the confusion, there had still been time for Jasper to vanish, but he's steadfastly refused to leave Snow's side. They'd cuffed and taken Jasper to the 26th Precinct and locked him in a cell by himself, but across from a cell filled with adults. One of the grown men had been Blaze.

❧

A blaring car horn, brought Total back to the real world. Somebody wanted to get into the parking space he'd been idling in front of. Nodding his head at the driver through the side mirror in understanding, he waited until there was a break in the traffic and pulled off. It was time to have a serious talk with Snow...there was some planning and killing to be done. He could feel it flowing through his veins.

Chapter 7

"That's five and..."

"Still nothing," Clay Edwards said finishing his partner's sentence. They'd been together almost fifteen years, but they'd known each other their entire lives. They'd started out stealing ten-speed bikes together, got caught together and entered a program for first-time juvies together. As a team, they'd entered the police academy and graduated twelfth and twenty-ninth out of their class. They'd both made detective very quickly. Washington while working narcotics and Clay while working with the Burglary Squad. They'd trailed each other into the homicide division and the natural course of events put them together as partners.

"We're using up an awful lot of IOU's on this," Wash said slamming the car door closed and rubbing his huge hands together

"Cold huh?"

"Than a motherfucker!" Wash reached out and angled one of the heating vents in his direction and leaned forward trying to restore the heat he'd lost, meeting one of his snitches.

"We could be foot patrol."

"We could be out with the flu too...no fucking way I'd be out in that shit walking!"

"So, what's next?" Clay asked watching the sidewalks behind them through the side view mirror.

"We watch and wait."

"Where?"

"Somewhere hot and toasty," Wash replied limbering up his fingers and then starting the unmarked car.

"You really think he'll show up in the City?" Clay asked as he spun his Yankee fitted cap backwards on his head.

"If he's smart as he seems to be he won't." Wash made a quick U-turn so they were on the downtown side of 8th Avenue.

"And if he ain't?"

"That's what our people are worried about."

"And?"

"We get between him and Trench."

"Bread and butter," Clay murmured as Wash hit the siren and the flashing rear and front lights, to keep from having to stop as the light at 110th Street turned red.

"Yeah, bread and butter," Wash repeated as Clay

leaned forward and began sampling a beat on the dash with his fingertips.

"Bread and butter...bread and butter..." Clay muttered bobbing his head.

Wash drove thinking, still wondering why the lieutenant had people not just from homicide on Total, but at least four cops each from Bunco, burglary and narcotics. Total was wanted for escape and the idiots that had allowed him to get away from the funeral parlor in Albany by rights, should be the ones doing the groundhog work. Sure Total's pops had been killed, but that surely hadn't been enough reason for them not to check the casket before they let him go down to pay his last respects. Gun, or no gun, somebody was going to be taking a long leave of absence without pay.

Wash turned onto 42nd and then made a quick left onto a side street next to Grand Central Station. A dozen marked and unmarked cars were already parked. It was a designated parking area for police.

"Looks hot and toasty from here," Clay said peering out the car window towards the huge glass windows of the station.

Wash could see the unasked question in his partner's eyes. "He got away in Albany right?" Clay nodded. "Then it's probable... I'm not guaranteeing it, but the likelihood exist that he might be dumb enough to come into the City by train."

A smile spread across Clay's full lips and he

reached for the door. "Damn you're smart!"

"Yeah I know," Wash replied to Clay's back and then jumped out the car and ran into the brightly lit station.

Chapter 8

"What kind of shit are we running?" Ace Lake demanded. He looked first at his own people, that had been with him for the past fifteen...sixteen years, then at his sons' "*peeps*" as they called them. Everybody that had been with Ace since the beginning, were in their late forties, early fifties like him. Where Ting-a-ling, and Birdie's crew were barely into their twenties. Ace's people wore dress clothes and listened to "*Oldies but Goodies*," while his sons' wore Gucci...Eoca Wear and listened to Fifty Cent, JaRule and old school Biggie Small's. He still regretted not letting his sons go out and do them, instead of pulling them into his own fold. Nobody said anything, even though there was a lot of shoulder shrugging.

"We got twenty-grand out on Snow," he said continuing. "And fifty on Total, now that he's out here and nobody can place them anywhere in Harlem. The nigga is bad news, but ain't no way everybody's supposed to be that scared.

"You forgot Trench put up another fifty," Ting-a-ling tossed in. "Now that nigga got reason to be scared!" there was giggling.

"Yeah and he needs to find that nigga worse than we do...his beef with us is business...that shit with Trench is personal." Ace picked up his drink, swirled the contents and tossed it back.

"So, what we gonna do?" Birdie asked looking at Tung-a-ling first and then their father.

"We can't even be sure Total's still down with Snow, but there's no sense taking no chances. We got three days to find them...if we don't, I got people coming in from St. Louis that will," Ace replied, then moved over to the conference table where three crystal decanters sat and poured himself another drink.

"I say fuck those St. Louis niggas! If they coming it's about getting in our pockets and I ain't feeling it!" Ting-a-ling said angrily. Turning to look at his younger brother, he raised his shoulders in a "What's up" gesture.

"Ting's, right Dad, they're our family and all but you know they been trying to get a piece of the pie for years...they handle our business and they're in there!"

"That's why it's business," Ace said. "We hit them off; they take care of their business and grab the first thing smokin' back home.

"What we hittin' off with?" Ting-a-ling asked.

"Whatever I feed 'em it's coming out of y'all

pockets, just like having to move to another spot." Ace looked directly at his sons' crew. "If somebody hadn't got cute with Alex and Drew, all our problems with Total would be in the wind.

"That nigga Drew acted like he wanted it, so we gave it to him right then...Fuck waiting!"

"And that's why your cousin's gonna be in a wheelchair the rest of his life!" Ace snarled. Chi-low frowned.

It had been simple. When Alex and Drew walked in, somebody put guns to their heads and ride them somewhere dark and lonesome. Instead, they'd started arguing with them about the prices they were being forced to pay for the coke and one thing had lead to another. Drew, more like his father than Alex had pulled his gun as they were pulling theirs and the whole thing had turned into a running gunfight. Not only had they missed the money from the other pickups, but they'd had to desert the spot.

Chi-low started to say something else feeling slighted, but Birdie cut him off. "What I want to know, is who's got nuts big enough to hide Snow when they know we're looking for her. What's it been, three...four weeks?"

"She could be out of the picture," Ting-a-ling suggested half-heartedly.

"She might have split, but she was in one piece according to her cousin," Birdie told them.

"How you manage that?" Ace asked, pouring another drink.

"Pop, that's his baby's momma! That bitch would sell out her whole family for Birdie!" Ting-a-ling said and then laughed. The rest of the crew joined in and Birdie sat back holding his tongue.

"Whatever, we need to try and handle this before Sunday. We know ain't none of the crew her brothers were running is still around. Like Birdie said, the question is, who's got the balls to hold out on us?" Ace lit a Newport.

Nobody could come up with an answer. True, Total had been strong enough when he first went to prison, to be able to reach out and get a couple of would-be stickup kids touched for robbing one of Snow's workers, but it shouldn't be enough to keep some crackhead or dopefiend needing a hit, or fix from giving them up on the down-low.

"Ting-a-ling...put some pressure on some of those niggas and their bitches," Ace said and turned to Brice one of his most trusted niggas. "You reach out and have a talk with Trench...don't personally like that lil' nigga, but maybe if we put our heads together we can get something done. This shit needs to be squashed!"

"*Yeah, for sure!*" Ting-a-ling thought and could see the same exact thoughts running through his brother's head, as they both watched their father pour his fourth double in less than thirty minutes.

Ace might be able to front on his squad, but they knew Ace was scared shitless and there wasn't room at the top for a scared motherfucker, whose heart pumped Kool-Aid.

Chapter 9

Parking Blaze's Caddy on 25th Street, Total punched a number into Snow's phone. The phone rang three times, before it was picked up and a sleepy voice answered.

"Chunky?" Total asked glancing at his watch and seeing that it was after one in the afternoon.

"All day partner," Chunky replied sounding a bit more awake.

"It's Total."

"Just caught onto that dog....What's up?"

"Got bigger fish to fry, than I can handle alone," Total replied, pulling a pack of smokes from the sunvisor.

"I'm listening."

"They're playing hardball."

"How hard?" Chunky asked.

"A hundred large for a head."

"Must be yours! You got some people seriously

scared!"

"Fo' sure!"

"They holding that long?"

"Way longer than that Chunky," Total replied finally deciding to light the smoke he'd been fucking with.

"Think it could be pried loose?"

"Like opening a crackhead soup!" Total replied, then giggled at the cigarette having made him drunk. He opened the window and tossed it. "So what's up?"

"You already know dog!"

"You coming personally?"

"Fo' you dog... only you. When and where?" Chunky asked. Total heard a female's voice ask Chunky if he wanted her to cook something to eat in the background .

"*Still Chunky*," Total thought and then told him where they'd touch base.

"It's a ride from Buffalo. . .I'll call you when we get in and work it from there."

"Almost like the old days at El and the Burn," Total said a loud and Chunky laughed.

"Could come close, but no cigar."

"See you when you get here!" Total tossed and snapped the phone closed.

******

"You know what you're doing Total?" Blaze

asked, after Total had filled him. in.

"Can't trust but a few people in the City with that kind of money being spread around."

"But you trust those people?"

"I'm out here ain't I?"

"Enough said," Blaze replied.

"When Snow finishes showering, y'all out of here...don't want her anywhere they can reach her, when I start this up." Total explained.

"Brooklyn?" Blaze asked and Total nodded. "Sure you don't need me to go along and hold your hand?" Blaze asked and gave a short laugh, but concern was written all over his face.

"I got two bikes, but I don't think both of them together would carry you to the nearest subway," Total replied smiling. "Besides, I'm only delivering a message...give them something to digest... get a couple of them to lose heart and make it a whole lot easier."

Blaze smiled outwardly, but inside he felt an emptiness in the center of his chest. He knew Total better than he knew himself and he knew, Total didn't just leave messages. What he did was get and keep your attention, which meant somebody or some bodies were going on a one-way trip. He didn't have it in him, to work any other way.

Snow's knock made Total turn towards the door and for the first time in his life, Blaze wished that he was forty, even thirty years younger. The 21st Century, was a time to be young...to be old and forced--not by lack of heart--to sit on the sidelines instead of being in the mix, made for old, jealous niggas and gangsters.

Total opened the door and snow dropped everything she was carrying at the sight of him and stepped into his arms.

Chapter 10

Dressed in full leathers, Total guided the 1999 Suzuki Hayabusa out of the storage shed. Dropping the kickstand, he went back over to the unit and took a couple minutes looking over his past life. Like the bike, Snow had taken everything that was of any value from his "*personal*" crib and put it in storage after he'd been found guilty. Twice a month, it had been her job to come out to the storage unit and bring out the bikes. She didn't ride...didn't even like motorcycles, but she'd start them and let them run for at least a good hour to keep them blowed out and running.

Locking the huge shed, Total climbed onto the bike and hit the starter. It came to life instantly, rumbling beneath him. "My baby!" Total mumbled, thinking of Snow.

Total knew that, what he intended was risky, but that was what life was all about. He knew that it would be at least another hour before Trench's hoods opened the dope spot, so he took the bike out along the Westside Highway and got back acquainted with it. It had been years, but every muscle and fiber of his body reacted like it had been just days before he'd been on the bike. Satisfied that he hadn't lost anything, Total headed for the heart of Harlem.

Total rode by the dope spot just in time to see seven women being herded inside the building. He knew they were the cutters and baggers. In ten minutes they'd be butt-naked and hard at work preparing dime bags of heroin that would be sold elsewhere.

Slowing his roll, Total cut across to 8th Avenue and spent twenty minutes just taking in the sights of what had once been his old hood. It was strange, that in a hood where heroin had been king, that most of the dealers were selling crack. The crackheads were making buys and hurrying to the nearest doorway, or phone booth and blazing up, not giving a fuck whether there were uniformed or detectives cruising through the avenues.

Returning to the area of Trench's operation, Total turned into the block and cut the engine. Using his booted feet, he guided the motorcycle up onto the sidewalk and in between the two buildings that rear ended the one he wanted in the next block.

Turning the bike so it was pointed back out of the alleyway, he leaned it against one of the buildings in the deep shadows and unfastened the saddlebag closest to him.

From the bag, he pulled the Smith and Wesson 9mm with the silencer reattached. Cocking it, he sat it down long enough to unzip his jacket, just in case he needed to get to the Desert Eagle it concealed. His message was to be a silent one, but the immediate future couldn't be predicted.

Moving quietly into the dark empty backyard and to the hole in the fence, he stepped through and took to the shadows to take inventory of his surroundings. Sure he was alone, he went to the fire escape ladder and climbed it as fast as he could without making any noise.

On the roof, Total eased open the door and peeked inside. There was nobody there. Stepping inside, he pressed his back against the stairwell wall and moved sideways down it, until he reached the fifth floor landing. Two of Trench's security people were too busy soft-rolling a pair of dice to even notice his presence above them. Their bad!

Headshots were the hardest, but after the first one slumped to the floor, the other went dead still, the dice in his hand--arm raised--as he was preparing to blow on them. Total pulled the trigger twice, as the man's head turned and his mouth falling open at the sight of the helmeted figure standing above him. The first round entered his mouth, as it fell open...the second created an all-seeing third eye in his forehead.

The next guard on the landing below was pissing, into a Star-buck's coffee cup. Total let him finish and shot him through the side of his head as he bent to sit the cup down.

Looking towards the door to the apartment where he knew drugs were being bagged up, Total was tempted to kick in the door and make a bigger mess. The deciding factor, were the Simmon brothers, who oversaw the bagging operation in Trench's stead. There was no way to know where they'd be inside the apartment and they were "*foreal*" killers. "*Messages*" Total thought and continued on down the staircase.

Sitting hunched over on the landing between the second and first floor, was the last inside guard. He sat, so he could see through the railing and spot anyone coming in the front door, that didn't belong. Beside him, was a cell phone, that all he need do was press a single digit that would ring the phone in the apartment and give the Siramon brothers plenty time to get ready for whatever.

Total creeped as close as he could get, peeked beyond the guard's shoulder at the front door and not seeing anyone he pulled the trigger three times. Three soft phfttts. The guard rolled down the steps and landed face up. There was no doubt, that the man was dead, but Total put an additional bullet in his skull. His eyes were open and Total wasn't chancing that there was even the tiniest bit of life left in his brain.

Sitting the gun down on the dead man's chest, Total jogged down the stairs to the first floor and walked the corridor to the door and slipped out the building and into the alleyway. He'd seen the two men sitting across the street in the running SUV, but neither had been looking his way.

The motorcycle was just as he left it. Pushing it back out of the alleyway and into the street, he zipped his jacket and climbed on.

"*Message delivered*" Total thought, as he brought the bike to life. It was going to be a long, cold ride to Brooklyn and Snow.

Chapter 11

Blaze sat on the living room couch, his eyes closed while Snow paced the straightaway between the living room and the kitchen at the back of the house. Every three to five minutes she would glance at her thin, diamond-studded watch and, then at her new Dolce & Gabbana designed Iphone, like doing so would make the motherfucker ring. It was going on two o'clock in the morning and it had been three-plus hours since Total had been in touch with them. She was tempted to dial the numbers of her old phone, but Total had it and it could fuck something up.

"He's okay and he'll be here soon enough," Blaze muttered sleepily. "You might as well go up and get some rest," he added purposely, not mentioning the triple vibration of the phone in his pocket that had woke him up. It was a new phone and only Total and Snow knew the numbers. Total had promised to give him a triple buzz, when he was definitely on his way out of Harlem.

"You think so?" Snow asked frowning at her celly. Blaze nodded. Turning, Snow made her way to the staircase. One heavy footstep after another, she made her way up to the second floor.

Entering the second of the row of three bedrooms, she moved to the bed, leaving the door open so she'd be able to hear Total when he came in. Timberlands still on, she hopped up onto the bed and stuffed the pillows behind her head sighing.

Snow's brain kept telling her, that Total was okay and that he knew exactly what he was doing--hadn't he come to her?--but she couldn't help but worry about him. She'd been worrying and loving him for too many years and habits were hard to break. Seventeen years of it and it didn't get any easier, even though he'd been only thirteen when it all really began.

❧

Drew had brought word that the BCS (Bureau of Children's Services) were making their way through the building, pounding on everybody's door. Snow had gone to the door and sat down to wait for them to reach her's.

"We're from Children's Services," one of the two suited men said, when Snow opened the door to the length of the security chain and peeked out. "We're doing a house to house....Do you know the Jefferies from the third floor?" Snow knew it was senseless to lie, so she nodded her head. We've got all the kids but the oldest boy Jasper...you wouldn't have happened to seen him around, or have any idea where he might go would you?"

"I used to see him and his brothers and sister around, but I really don't know him. I was in a couple of classes with his sister Beverly," Snow told them.

"We really need to find him...the other kids have been placed and we'd like to see Jasper placed somewhere off the streets," the speaker said pulling a business card from inside the jacket of his suit and sticking it through the gap of the chained door.

Snow took the card and pretended to study the information on it.

"You see him, or hear anything give us a call," the second man told her.

"No problem," Snow replied and closed the door. When Snow turned Jasper was standing there, tears in his big eyes.

"They split us up the last time he went to jail," Jasper said sobbing silently.

"I know and I won't let them get you," Snow replied and ran her fingers across his beady head.

"Promise?" Jasper had asked in a whisper.

"No Jasper...I swear on it!"

"Love you Snow," Jasper muttered and wrapped his arms around the tops of Snow's thighs hugging her tightly.

They'd stood that way for fifteen minutes a truly odd couple... him almost thirteen and Snow recently turned sixteen...him a tad over five-foot and Snow the six-feet she'd stop growing at.

Even so young, they'd both been wise enough to know the shit the BCS guys were talking was bullshit. They knew they wouldn't stop looking. Jasper's father had finally crossed the ultimate line. He'd gotten dusted up on the garbage he was supposed to be selling and in a fit of rage, he'd beaten Jasper's mother to death with a hammer.

Because the BCS didn't want to give up their search and some big-mouthed neighbor had told them about his and Snow's friendship, Jasper had taken to riding the trains or hiding in the tunnels during the daytime and then coming back to the building after it was dark. The roof landing became his hideout and most times when he showed up, Snow was already there waiting on him.

Snow would bring blankets, a pillow and food from her house, but most importantly she came with books and herself. They'd eat together first and then Snow would open one of the books and teach him whatever she had learned that day. Sometimes they'd sit and talk and when they talked, Jasper's age became a non-factor. It was during one of those talks, that they'd found themselves staring wordlessly into each other's eyes. Nothing had ever been said, but they'd both known in their minds and hearts, that they'd been destined for each other.

It might have gone on forever, if big stupid Noonie hadn't tried to take advantage of Jasper, one day when he was waiting for Snow to show up at the Midtown game room. Snow had shown up while Noonie was trying to run Jasper's pockets. Jasper was putting up a silent fight, but at ninety-five pounds, he wasn't close to being a match for Noonie at two-hundred pounds. Snow had snuffed Noonie in her eye and while Noonie wailed about being blind, Snow had kicked her ass up until the owner and security broke it up. They'd made Snow and Jasper leave first at the threat of calling the police.

Chapter 12

Two blocks from the crib, the phone Total had gotten from Snow vibrated in his pocket. Pulling the motorcycle over to the curb, he pulled the phone out, making a note to cop one of the Blue Tooth's Blaze and Snow used so his hands would always be free.

"Holla partner!" came Chunky's familiar drawl.

"You made it huh?"

"All day and lovin' it dog!"

"Where you at right now?" Total asked checking the time.

"Times Square and feeling it...we doing this shit New Years fo' sure!"

Total smiled, hearing the excitement in Chunky's usually cool, calm, and collected matter along with the laughter and whistles in the background.

"There's a McDonalds on 42nd Street that lays open all night...I can meet you there in an hour, or you can cruise down to 28th Street, between 7th and

8th Avenues...got a club down there called "*Shadows*," that rocks until daybreak. Same time frame, but you and your peeps can chill out...maybe catch a few late night New York shorties to keep you company 'til I show," Total explained and heard Chunky relay the options. In unison, he heard "Shadows!"

"Know you felt that dog!" Chunky said.

"I'll be there in an hour and whatever it is, it's on me."

"See you when you get there!" Chunky called and the line went dead.

Total snapped the phone closed and rolled away from the curb, just as a police car turned into the block. He made a left ahead of them and rode four blocks before he headed back and to the house.

Total had intended to bring Chunky and his crew down to the Brooklyn spot, but he'd thought better on it. There was Snow and Blaze to consider. Chunky was his man for sure and had been since the second day he'd climbed off the bus from Downstate at Auburn. They'd been in the chow hall, when Chunky spit straight into one of the guards' faces. The guard had pulled the pin on his alarm and the shit had gotten funky. They'd come twenty deep from the door for Chunky and found like nine of Chunky's homies and Total standing in the way. The first battle they'd won, but it wasn't happening again after they flooded the chow hall with close to fifty guards. Chunky and Total had wound up in cells next to each other--after they'd been cut loose from the hospital--and Chunky had asked him one question. "Why?" Total had replied simply, that the next one they came for could be him and they'd been tight every since. The problem was that he didn't know who Chunky was bringing and until he did, the existence of the house, Snow and Blaze was in limbo. He'd chance putting himself out there, but not them.

Riding up onto the sidewalk in front of the house, Total was about to turn off the bike, when Blaze opened the door and came down the steps.

"I gotta go back out, I just got a call from my people from Buffalo," Total said.

"Man, that's on you!" Blaze told him and glanced towards the house. "She's been squatting on you all night...I finally got her to go to bed after you beeped me."

"She sleep?" Total asked and Blaze nodded. "Shit!" Total hissed.

"What's the problem?"

"I need to get some money from her."

"Let her sleep, 'til you're ready to talk to her," Blaze said and dug into the inside pocket of his sports coat. He pulled out first one rubber banded roll of bills and then a second. "It's three-grand...you need more than that? I'll have to go to my bank," he added and handed Total the money.

"Naw, this will work!" Total stuck the money in his jacket pocket and zipped it.

"What will I tell her when she wakes up?"

"Tell her I was here...didn't want to wake her." Total reached behind him and undid the saddlebag. Pulling out an unwrapped bottle of wine, he handed it to Blaze.

"Can't pronounce it, but I know what this shit cost. No wonder you're broke!" Blaze joked.

"Chateau...Le...Pin...Pomerol. Give it to her and tell her I said to put it on ice and that I'll be back before it gets too cold," Total said and began rolling the motorcycle backwards and towards the street.

"Be sure you do that, I'm not feeling sleeping out on the porch," Blaze replied and started up the steps sideways.

"I got you," Total said trying to keep from laughing.

Total took 6th Avenue up to 29th Street and rode it until he came to the parking lot between 7th and 8th. Cruising through the lot, he stopped when he could see up along 28th Street where the club was. There were people moving up and down the block, mostly in pairs with the results of a good night plastered to their faces. Midway up the block and across the street from Shadows, was a crowd of maybe thirty to forty people--mostly women. They stood on the sidewalk side between two identical, black 1968 Chevy Impalas, cheering and screaming as the cars' hydraulics were being put through their paces as Fifty Cent's *Technology* blasted from unseen speakers.

He'd found the Buffalo crew.

Closer to him against the wall stood Chunky. He had an arm wrapped around the sides of a shorty, she was wearing a mini and a short fur coat that she knew damn well it was too cold for. His gloved hands against the wall behind her, kept her hostage, but she didn't seem to want to be anyplace else as Chunky whispered into her ear and she fucked with his dick.

Pulling out of the parking lot after unzipping his jacket, Total rode the bike until he was positioned right behind Chunky. Cutting the engine, he sat straddling the bike.

One of Chunky's hands seemed to float down from its position on the wall, as he glanced over his shoulder and shifted his body ever so slightly. Total waited until the hand disappeared beneath the tail of the long, mink-collared leather coat and then flipped up the visor on his helmet and made himself known.

Chunky's hand reappeared, dipped into his coat pocket and came out holding a cell phone. "Put your digits in my phone," he told the girl as he came away from the wall and walked towards Total his coattail flapping with the slick motion of his hands.

"What's up?" Total asked.

"You dog!" Chunky said and wrapped his long arms around Total's back and shoulders, hugging him hard.

"Much love," Total replied hugging Chunky back.

"Nothing but," Chunky whispered as they parted.

"You ain't changed," Total said lowering his voice, as he motioned to where the girl stood hold Chunky's phone a hand on an arched hip. It was obvious from the look on her pretty face, that she felt that any hugging that was done should've been between her and Chunky.

"In the genes," Chunky replied, then added. "Let me get my celly for baby takes a walk with it... know these New York City whores be scandalous!" He said it loud enough so she'd hear it and still she accepted him, when he pulled her up against him and whispered against her ear. Handing Chunky the phone, shorty went up on her toes and planted a wet one on his lips. A glance over at Total and she headed up the street fat ass swinging.

Sticking two fingers into his mouth, Chunky whistled loudly. The car show shut down, as the niggas inside the cars came out and moved along with two others that had been mingling with the crowd in their direction. A fifth backed up from where he'd been standing and played the wall his eyes shifting to take in the ends of the blocks.

"Duke...Reddog...Checkmate...Gunz," Chunky said motioning at each one with a pocketed hand. Each acknowledge the intro with a slight nod. "This is the nigga I was telling y'all 'bout...this is Total-E."

"What's up?" Total responded, then looked back

up the block. "Who's that with the screw face?" he asked.

Chunky smiled showing all his teeth through a crooked smile. "That's my left hand Murder Nth."

"Remember you from Clinton," Gunz threw in.

Total cocked his head for a dozen ticks. "Third court over and one up from mine's," Total pushed and Gunz smiled and nodded his head.

"So what we 'bout to be up to?" Chunky asked, squatting and fanning his tailcoat halves back out the way as he began examining the bikes engine.

"*Same old Chunky...always a ratchet in reach,*" Total thought catching a glimpse of the Glock 9mm at Chunky's waist.

"Tonight's R&R (Rest and Relaxation)." Total pulled out the rolls of money he'd gotten from Blaze and handed them to Chunky. Chunky dropped the money into his pockets without even looking at it. "You already found some hookers... there's two hotels along 8th Avenue before you get to 34th Street. Pick one and when your crew has recuperated sometime tomorrow, give me a call and we'll get together and go over things," Total finished.

"I'm feeling that!" Chunky stated as he stood and turned to face his people, that were half-mooned behind him. "Y'all feeling it or what?" he asked and everybody nodded, then turned and headed back up the street to the cars and bitches.

"What about Murder?" Total asked as he keyed

the ignition and started the bike.

"Told you, he's my left...Where you gonna be?" Chunky asked pulling out his phone.

"Close," Total replied and revved the bike.

"Wheelie that motherfucker!" Chunky said, then began punching numbers into his phone as he walked sideways towards his crew.

Total revved the bike several times and then streaked down the block. Just before he reached the cars, he raised up the frontend and rode it until he reached the corner. Even through the helmet and all the noise, he could hear Chunky shouting, "My nigga!" over and over again.

Chapter 13

Having first making a quick phone call to Blaze and learning that he was still holding the bottle of wine he'd left for Snow--which meant she was still asleep--Total checked the bike into the Meyer's parking lot next to Madison Square Garden and walked over to where he caught the D-train to 125th Street.

Out of old habits, Total tried to exit at 127th Street and found the way blocked off. Heading back, he exited at 125th and made his way to 8th Avenue against a freezing wind. Taking a left, he spotted the end building of the St. Nick projects and a smile creped onto his lips despite the cold.

It had been a long time since he'd even stepped foot into the projects, but the closer he came the more it seemed like he was coming home. There were three people in the courtyard of his old building, but he didn't recognize them. He however did recognize their moves and mannerisms. They were lookout/

streeters and they were watching for the police and any late night customers. One of them moved to intercept Total, then got a good look at him as he raised his head and made a U-turn.

Pulling one of the double doors open, Total stepped into the surprising warmth of the hallway and looked straight into a face from a long, distant past. Noonie stood in the doorway leading to the front stairs. Two other people along with her stared at him, and followed his progress towards the elevators with their eyes. Glancing back, Total saw them turn and look back towards the doors of the building and outside. The elevator rattled to a stop and Total climbed in, glad that Noonie hadn't recognized him.

◆

As good three minutes passed, before Noonie spun around and ran to the elevators. She glanced up at the lit floor-number display and saw that the elevator had stopped on five.

"Ficking shit, I'm losing it" Noonie cried.

"What the fuck are you talking about?" Rayford demanded, looking back and forth between his sister and Granger their package man. "You been smoking without me?"

"Fuck smoking! It's him! Thank God!" Noonie clapped her hands together as if she was in church and the spirit had hit her.

"What the fuck are you talking about? Who... who the fuck is him," Rayford asked yet again.

Noonie ignored her brother, ran a few steps over so she could see the nook in the lobby and cussed. "That little shit took off with the package!" she snarled angrily, then moved back to the elevator and began watching the display.

"We're fucked!" Rayford said, his shoulders slumping.

"Naw lil' nigga, we just came up...."Where's the gun Ray?" Noonie asked holding out her hand. Undoing his coat, Rayford took the old .38 snub-nosed revolver from the back of his pants and handed it to her.

"We..we ain't gonna catch Granger tonight...not with almost a whole fifty-pack."

"It ain't for "G" stupid, it's for him. Told you we was on the come-up!"

"Who Noonie? Who...who's him?" Rayford asked, as he found his eyes watching the floor indicator along with his sister.

"That nigga Jasper!" Noonie said bobbing her head and wishing she could chance going to the steps and taking a hit of crack, before he came down.

"You talkin' about Total?"

"Total...Jasper, same low-life motherfucker!" Noonie hissed and found her fingers caressing the inch-wide section of the scar on her face. "We bagging that nigga," she added, then took a deep breath as she cocked the gun's hammer.

"Gimme a quarter...I'm...I'm calling somebody. If you fo' sure it's him."

"You ain't calling nobody nigga! We call and they send somebody, who you think is going to collect the money?" Noonie asked, taking her eyes off the indicator a split second.

"But..."

"But shit! Too late anyway, elevator's coming down. You just be ready to snatch open that door when it gets here'. ..fuck it up and I'm going to use this on you!" she growled and aimed the gun at her brother just to let him know she wasn't having it.

Rayford hesitated only a split second and moved to the elevator, catching the handle.

Noonie watched the lights lighting up from number to number as the elevator descended. Three... two...one...lobby. The elevator shook to a stop and Rayford snatched the door open and moved sideways so he could see.

Big Noonie smiled a split second--for the first time in years that she could remember--before she began pulling the trigger. The three gunshots reverberated and echoed through the empty lobby as Total was slammed backwards into the elevator.

"I told you...told you it was him!" Open that fucking door and let's see who's smiling this time!" Noonie screamed, her eyes the size of pool balls.

Looking like he was ready to cry, run, or both,

Rayford pushed himself up from his crouch where he'd been holding his ears and opened the door.

From the floor, Total pulled the trigger three times. The roar of the Desert Eagle made Noonie's shots sound like fake firecrackers.

Noonie no longer looked amused, as the first shot gouged out a chunk of fat from her stomach and sent her crashing backwards into the lobby wall. The second shot, tore into the flesh of her throat. The gun dropped from her hand as she raised it to claw at the heat in her throat. Blood seeped through and over her fingers, as she slid lifelessly to the filthy hallway floor.

The last round tore two fingers off Rayford's hand as he tried to shield himself and buried itself in his chest, but Rayford was far from stupid. He was running before Noonie's body hit the floor.

Shoving himself up, Total pushed the elevator door opened and jumped out. Spotting the splatters of blood that turned into a trail, he followed them out onto the back steps.

Rayford lay curled up against the padlocked basement door. Tears" ran down his thin cheeks leaving another trail as they carried away two weeks worth of dirt.

"Wasn't...wasn't...wasn't my idea," Rayford slobbered holding his hand against his chest.

"Wasn't mine either," Total said calmly and pulled the trigger twice, almost taking of Rayford's head.

Running back up the stairs, Total ducked out the back door. He didn't allow the sounds of approaching sirens to hurry him as he searched the parking lot. Spotting the Audi, he walked to it and unlocked the door. Pulling the backpack from his shoulders, he tossed it across the seat and climbed in behind the wheel.

Taking his time, Total drove out the 7th Avenue end of the lot and made a left heading Uptown. At 145th Street, he made a right and headed towards the East River.

Sure he was out of the immediate area, Total dug beneath his clothes locating first one and then the other two bullets from Noonie's gun, buried in the mesh of the Kevlar vest. He wasn't leaking, but he'd have serious bruises for the next few weeks. Once again, he found himself truly owing Blaze, but it was better than being planted.

Chapter 14

They'd been driving for better than an hour after leaving New York and the landscape kept getting more and more rugged. Every five minutes or so, Snow found herself staring at Total. He'd showed up after five in the morning and though she was awake, she pretended to be sleep. Even when he stripped naked and slid beneath the covers next to her already naked body. He had curled up against her--an arm across her body so he could cup one of her breast—and the hardest part was ignoring him when his dick grew almost instantly hard and pressed against her upper thighs. The only consolation in punishing him, for staying out all night and not calling, was that the tiny bit of doubt that had grown in her mind that he'd been with another woman vanished.

"Find somewhere I can pee," Snow muttered. A few minutes later, Total pulled the car over into a rest area and nodded toward the brick building with stick drawings of a man and woman on the two doors. "I'm not going in there by myself," Snow told him as she climbed from the car. Total got out behind her and walked over to the door she'd entered.

"You okay?" he called.

"No! Get in here!" Snow shouted in reply.

Looking around, Total sheepishly pushed the door open and stepped inside; praying that some woman traveler didn't suddenly developed a need to go while he was inside.

"Okay now? I'm here," Total half whispered, looking around.

"Come here," she called and Total moved over to the stalls.

Seeing his feet, Snow finished pulling down her tight jeans and panties, then bent across the toilet her ass facing the door.

"Inside!"

Shaking his head, Total pushed the door open and found himself looking at nothing but ass and the sliver of pink that showed between the dark lips of Snow's fat-lipped pussy. Even with him knowing that it wasn't the right place or time, Total found his dick growing hard.

"We're going to jail!" he said, stepping into the cubicle and undoing first his coat and then his jeans. Stepping close to Snow, he felt the heat from her body against his groin and thighs. Taking a half step back, he pushed her short jacket up so he could stroke her sides.

"If you take all day...we might just go to jail," Snow stated as she spread her feet as far apart as they would within the confines of the jeans down around her calves.

Total ran both hands down from the silkiness of her sides to the even softer curves of her hips and ass.

"This is crazy," he whispered, stroking Snow's shaved pussy with the tips of his fingers. When he felt the wetness, he knew this had been her intent from the start. Parting the lips of her pussy, so he could examine the complete pinkness and the small, mouth-like opening of her fuck hole, he pressed two fingers into the juicy opening and felt it clamp down on them.

A shiver ran through Snow's body, as Total's fingers moved deftly in and out of her. Against her conscious will, she found herself rolling her pussy to meet each of his thrust. In minutes, she was panting and sucking at the bathroom's stale air.

"Don't ever stay away from me like... like that again!" she squealed and double roll her pussy onto his fingers.

Pulling his fingers out, Total guided the head of his dick into Snow. She reached back, caught the thickness of his dick and shoved herself back onto it, then put her hand back on the wall. Total withdrew until just the head lay inside Snow's wetness and then fucked into her with everything he had, causing her to gasp.

"No baby... don't you ever pretend to be asleep on me again," he uttered in warning and began fucking back into her over and over, deeper and deeper.

"Won't...won't...arrrhh...swear to God!" Snow cried out as a wave of pure ecstasy surged through her body, making her head go light and her legs wobbly.

●

"So, are you going to tell me where we're going now?" Snow asked, as she leaned back with her head against the soft leather of the headrest, eyes closed. She stroked Total's thigh to the rhythm of Mary J. Blige crooning "No More Drama."

"To see an old friend of mine's and to pick up some stuff we need," Total replied, smiling as he recalled portions of what had happened twenty minutes before in the bathroom.

"And?"

"And what?"

"Why'd you bring me? You could have handled that by yourself."

Total remained quiet for several moments, then told her. "I need to know if you're ready to handle what we got to handle. If I don't know, I can't do me without worrying if you're good."

"And if you think I'm not?"

"You still got a babysitter," Total answered, his voice almost apologetic.

"You gave me your word!" Snow pulled her hand away and crossed her arms tightly across her chest.

"Ting-a-ling and his crew ain't nothing but the tail of the snake...you still get dibs on the head. I gave my word."

"You think he did my father?" Snow asked, knowing that the snake's head that Total was talking about, was Ace Lake. She dropped her hand back against his thigh and began caressing it.

Total opened his mouth to respond, then stopped as he reached to turn, up the radio as Little Wayne came on it. "A snake's a snake...his hand was in what happened to your brothers...snakes don't change, they keep doing them until you take off their heads," he finally said, his head rocking to the beat of the music. "We're here!" he added making a right turn of the highway and onto a dirt road partially lined with bare trees.

The trees end, as they topped a rise, from where they could see a large-framed house sitting alone in the valley below. Stopping the car, Total leaned on the horn three times. Two short and once long.

"You see that? Somebody looked out the door," Snow said and Total headed down the hill.

Total didn't bother to explain, that the simple look from the door meant two things. One, come on down. Two, come down and show yourself when you get here. Total wondered as he cruised down the hill toward the house whether Maximillian would recognize him, thru the dreads and beard. He didn't gamble anything but exercises, so he bet himself a hundred pushups the old man would. Pulling the car sideways across the front of the house, he killed the engine.

"Stay in the car till I call for you," Total instructed and took his time climbing from the car. "When I call you, bring the money with you," he added slamming the door and strolling up the short walkway.

Even though he couldn't find where Max was watching from, he knew without doubt that he was being observed. Nobody stayed in the game Max was in for close to forty years, without taking a single bust without being careful. If he wanted, Max could have lines at his house that looked like they were passing out welfare cheese. Instead, he chose only to deal with a "chosen" few. His favorite saying, was "*all money ain't good money*" and so far it had held true.

The door of the house opened as Total stepped up onto the porch and Max stood there, bracing himself with a cane. Unhooking the screen door, he turned and disappeared back inside without a single word. The cane forced a moment of thought and then Total turned and motioned for Snow.

Pulling the canvas bag from the floor of the backseat, Snow slid from the car and strode to the porch to join Total. He motioned her inside and followed, closing and locking the doors.

They stood in a huge living room with a massive

fire burning in the fireplace. Three Siamese cats lay curled up in front of it, two obviously asleep while the third groomed itself with its tongue and watched them through chinked eyes.

When Snow looked questioningly at Total, he winked and moved by her to take the lead. He led the way out of the living room, through a kitchen and to a door beneath the staircase that led up to the house's second and third floors.

"Watch your step," Total warned as he pushed the door open and stood aside for Snow to enter. He took the bag as she moved pass him.

At the bottom of the stairs, they made a right and travelled a good fifty feet, before they came to another door. This one opened. The inside of the door seemed to be padded. They went through it, with Total pulling it closed and sliding the two massive slide-bolts into place.

"Duck!" Total said, as he did himself. For twenty feet they walked bent over and then the room's ceiling rose, so that even standing Total wouldn't have been able to touch it.

The three walls that made up the remainder of the room were covered with sandbags to their ceilings.

"This can't be part of the house," Snow stated, looking around.

"You're perceptive...very perceptive!" A voice said from only a few feet away, then Max appeared from a section of the sandbagged walls that had been pushed outwards. Hobbling over to where Total stood, he wrapped his arms around him and pounded his back. "About time someone I like came to visit!"

Allowing the canvas bag to drop, Total returned the embrace. Beneath the new-looking suit with its slightly padded shoulders, Total could feel the old man's frailness. There was no sign of the muscularity he'd been used to. Time had surely been waging an ongoing war and Max was losing.

"So, introduce me to the wonderful lady," Max said, as they broke apart and he turned to face Snow straightening an unrumpled jacket. He stood with a rare smile on his withered lips, his hands folded atop the head of the cane.

"Maximillian...meet Snow," Total said and watched Max reach out a swollen-knuckled hand. Snow held out her hand and Max took it and bending from the waist, kissed the back of it.

"Finally," Max said straightening, but not relinquishing his hold. "I'm afraid you've been wrong all these years...she's not beautiful, she's exquisite! I think you did so to keep me at bay. You show up with her, when I'm just too old to do anything about it."

"Thank you Maximillian...Max," Snow responded, her eyes brighter than they normally were. It was obvious, that she was impressed,

"You'll never be that old," Total proclaimed, finding himself smiling at the scene. At the vibes.

With an audible sigh, Max gave Snow her hand

back. "So, what can I do for you two today? He asked taking a step back.

"I'll need at least nine Heckler & Koch 9-milimeters," Total told him.

"I can do four Hecklers', but the rest will have to be Sigs," Max informed Total and turned heading back towards the opening from which he had appeared.

"That much better, but I'll still need silencers and at least three extra clips per!" Total called out wanting to be sure Max would hear him behind the wall.

"Next?" Max called back.

"Crowd control....Got any suggestions?"

"MP..."

"Old school...nothing wrong with old school, but..." Total said cutting Max off and then finding himself served to a dose.

"The five yes, but not the MP-10!"

"Haven't had the pleasure" Total, confessed, his eyes on Snow.

"And, I have something you might be interested in...on the personal level," Max said as he re-entered the room pushing a speed cart, that was more at home in a kitchen or restaurant.

Rolling the cart to a stop beside Total and in front of Snow, Max picked up his cane and moved back a half-dozen steps.

Total looked beyond the Hecklers and Sigs, with which he was more than familiar and reached to pick up the chrome-plated semi-auto that lay among them.

It was a beautiful weapon, with grips that looked like bone. Keeping his eyes averted, he weighed the gun in his hand. It was slightly heavier than any 9mm he'd ever held, but wasn't any larger.

"A forty?" Total guessed, as he reached down and took one of the set of ear-protectors from the bottom shelf of the cart and pulled them on.

"See if you can tell after you test fire it," Max suggested, as he got Snow's attention with the tip of his cane and pointed at the other set of ear guards.

Snow picked up the guards and pulled them on, just as Total turned to tell her to. He smiled at Max, then turned and raised the gun towards the back wall. He squeezed the trigger once, then twice more still unable to figure the caliber out. Going down on one knee and holding the gun with both hands he squeezed the trigger until the weapon locked back on empty. Glancing at Max, he angled the weapon so he could read the stamp on the side of it.

"Ten millimeter...beautiful," he mused, then dropped the clip out into his hand and went back to the cart. Sitting them down, he again bent and went to the bottom shelf. This time picking up the MP-10 that rested there.

"Too glittery for him," Snow said smiling at Max.

"Thank you Miss-know-it-all, now come over here!" Total said, as he dropped the MP-10's clip into his hand and checked the load.

"Might have it in black matte in a few days," Max

offered, as he watched Total position himself behind Snow after slamming the thirty-round clip home.

"Not in my schedule Max," Total said, clicking the safety off the weapon and placing it in Snow's hands. "Keep it aimed at the floor until you're ready." The later directed at Snow. "Three-count pulls until it's empty." he stepped back.

The MP-10 was much heavier than anything Snow had ever fired, with the exception of one of her father's old shotguns. The double-barreled ones were really heavy. Raising and extending her arm, she caressed the trigger to a three-count pull, and then did it again and again until the weapon was empty.

"Stick out your hand," Total ordered, taking the MP from her. Snow stuck out her hand and it barely trembled. Snatching a pin-up target from the bottom of the cart, after returning the MP-10, Total walked to the far wall and hung it on one of the sandbags, chest high. Coming back, he chose one of the already silenced Sigs and gave it to Snow.

"What now?" Snow asked.

"You've got fifteen shots to hit three bulls' eyes... you do it, you roll with me...don't..." Total began but didn't finish, as Snow removed the safety, turned to the wall and began firing. She fired eight rounds one-handedly.

Dropping the clip, she cleared the chamber of the round that was in it and spoke to Total as he walked towards the target. "I go!" she said and winked at

Max as she sat the gun back on the cart.

"You go," Total replied examining the target. Three of the seven shot were bull's eyes, while the other four were outside the ring, he could cover them all with the palm of his hand.

Chapter 15

"Get us the fuck out of here!" Wash screamed as he jumped into the SUV and slammed the door.

"What the fuck's up?" Clay asked, even as he started the car.

"Fuckin' bodies and we're somewhere we ain't supposed to be!" Wash replied, digging out his phone and pressing a single digit. "Don't worry who the fuck it is!" he yelled as someone picked up the phone. "Just get your people and that shit out of that spot now! And don't come down the front steps...use the roof and go out the back!" he added and clicked the cell phone closed.

"Where to?" Clay asked.

"Make a right and hit Amsterdam...anywhere in Midtown is good," he answered, letting the window down and tossing the phone into the shadows.

"You crazy?"

"Don't worry it's a clone."

Clay drove until they crossed 59th Street and then headed across it until they hit Park Avenue, where he pulled over and parked in the first available spot.

"Explanation please?" Clay asked looking at the dumb look his partner wore.

"It's him...that sonuvabitch is here!" Wash said raising up so he could search his pockets for something.

"Who's here?"

"That Nigga Jefferies!"

"You saw him? Why the fuck did we run?"

"No I didn't see him and we weren't running," Wash said, just as his cell phone chirped. He flipped it open and listened after identifying himself. "We're at 59th and Park," he said into the phone. "Be there in twenty minutes." he swiveled the phone closed and tossed it onto the dashboard.

"We heading back right?" Clay asked and Wash nodded his head. "I'm listening," Clay said and restarted the car and hit the switch for the lights and siren.

"It's a good thing I wasn't peeing out in no fucking cold!" Wash said, as they watched two of the coroner's helpers making their way down the partially iced steps of the building across from where they were parked.

"You went to pee in the hall man?" Clay asked.

"Fucking right!" Wash said and Clay shook his head yet again.

"We can count our lucky stars that I had to go... and that I went inside to do it. We might have been sitting here when the first cops showed and there wouldn't have been shit that we could have said to justify us sitting across from a fucking dope spot, with four bodies in it."

"Yeah you're right." Clay stuck out his clenched, gloved fist and Wash tapped it with his own.

"We were right here man," Wash said, as yet another pair of the coroner's men made their way down the steps with another body-bagged gurney between them.

"I saw shit!"

"We saw shit!" Wash corrected. "I just don't figure why he split without running up in the spot."

"Somebody...something scared him off?"

"It ain't happening, that nigga ain't scared of jack!" Wash picked up the cup of coffee he'd been drinking from, sampled it and then opened the SUV's door wide enough to sling the cup beneath the vehicle.

"What now?"

"We go on the fucking offense."

"Explain that one?"

"We sit on everything that Trench owns...this time with our eyes wide open and when he raises his head again, we bag him!"

"That's a whole lot of shit to watch and it still leaves us sitting on our hands till he makes the move," Clay responded.

"We got all the backup we'll need. We put them on the spots where Trench ain't. We sleep with Trench if we have to."

"It would be nice if we could keep him alive until Christmas," Clay said starting the car, as the last of the body bags was being brought down the stairs and the Medical Examiner hurried towards the City's wagon.

"We need to do that...twenty thousand in bonus money will pay a lot of bills. Let's get to the station and get that paperwork done so we can pay our benefactor an up and close visit. I think we got a bonus coming anyway for saving him all that dope!"

"I feel that!" Clay replied and pulled away from the curb.

Chapter 16

It had taken less than an hour to locate Ting-a-ling's white Denali Parked on Manhattan Avenue. Total had intended to let Chunky, Gunz and Murder sit on it until Ting-a-ling appeared and then trail him wherever, but then Birdie had shown up and double-parked his silver Lexus. Instead of letting Chunky hang out, he'd called them on his cell phone and told them to ride shotgun on Birdie. Birdie had only stayed in the brownstone a couple minutes and when he pulled off, Chunky had pulled out behind him. Twenty minutes later, Total got his first look at Ting-a-ling.

"Piece of shit!" he murmured and allowed Ting-a-ling to hit 110th Street before he pulled out of his parking space and began trailing him in Blaze's Caddy.

"I could do him Total...pull up beside him and it's a cold wrap," Snow said, reaching beneath the seat and pulling out the huge .357 she'd gotten from Blaze to replace the .380 she'd had to dump.

"Ain't time Baby. We stick to the plan," Total replied. Snow looked at him, her plea clear in her eyes. Total shook his head "No" and she stuck the gun back beneath the seat, not really wanting to.

"We stick to the plan," she offered slouching back against the seat heated.

The meeting had been held in Chunky's suite at the Pennsylvania Hotel. Blaze had refused to be left behind again, so they'd all been there. The plan was a good one in its simplest. Since the Buffalo crew didn't know anybody that was involved, it was decided that Snow would be the pointer for the initial contact. Once the crew knew who they were hunting, they could act independently or if it was anything that looked like it would be a problem, they'd all roll together. But, even before the first move was made, they needed to find Ace Lake and his sons' other holes. A fox might roam all day, but sooner or later it returned to the place it felt safest.

Total hadn't put them down with his personal beef with Trench, because it was just that, *"personal."* He'd made the first contact at the dope bagging spot and he'd keep making them until he'd dismantled Trench's entire operation, or until he could personally slump him.

In four and a half hours, it became obvious that Ting-a-ling was making pickups. He'd climb out his truck, dip into a building or storefront and come back out within minutes carrying a bag he hadn't gone in with. The stores Total didn't want to chance, because they were small and he might walk right into Ting-a-ling, but he did trail him into three different buildings. He missed the location once, but found him twice and that was a good start.

It was late-night, when Ting-a-ling finally headed out of Harlem and towards the East side. Total followed him down second Avenue and over onto East 28th Street. From the Avenue, Total watched him park and activate the alarm, before climbing the steps of a very expensive looking Brownstone. Leaving Snow with the car, Total strolled into the block. There was only one name on the mailbox. Ace Lake Jr. Total smiled as he slipped back down the steps and headed to the car.

"Nigga clocking like the Feds!" he expressed, climbing into the car. "You got any idea how much he pulls down in a week?"

"At least a brick...Alex and Drew were hitting him with five-hundred grams every four days and he was still sneaking around and making deals with those Dominicans in Washington Heights," Snow told him and Total whistled.

"Think he might be stupid enough to keep that kind of money in his crib?"

"Possible...he was stupid enough to fuck with me. Where to?"

Total pulled out his cell phone and began punching numbers. "I need to check in with Chunky and see what he's working with. If it ain't nothing serious, we can head home."

"Think I'd better make a call too...I've had Keisha on hold a long time...let her know its dead," Snow said using her speed-dial

Total was positive that Snow was, opening the door for a talk they hadn't had, but he just wasn't ready for it. For seven years, of his nine in prison, Snow had gone through at least four girl-friends and had put him down on them. From the day they had let him out of the juvenile facility at eighteen, he and Snow had been fucking like bunnies. All the way up until the day they'd got him for the bodies in the Bronx, they'd fucked and sucked each other a minimum of twice a day, so there was no way he even expected her to just stop. He'd even told her it was okay to find her a nigga to keep her company, but she'd turned down the offer. Two years into his bid, she'd written and told him about her first "*girlfriend*" assuring him, that it was only a form, of release. She was always the aggressive one in her girl-girl relationships, but he knew that it was only so she would be in control.

Total's brain was floating back to the first night in Morningside Park, when Chunky answered the phone.

Chapter 17

Snow sat parked in the car waiting for Total's return. He'd said he would only be a minute, but twenty minutes had passed and he still wasn't back. She was just about to get out of the car, when Total came through the revolving side door of the Pennsylvania hotel accompanied by Chunky. Chunky waved to her and stepped back inside but didn't move.

"Something wrong?" Snow asked examining the expression on Total's face and not liking it, as he climbed into the passenger seat.

"Maybe, maybe not," he replied shifting so he could get into the pocket of his old Snorkel. He pulled out a cell phone Snow hadn't seen before. Opening it, he pressed several buttons and then held it so she could see it.

"That's Shawnee!" Snow said excitedly.

"Then something's wrong," Total replied and hit the button to shift the picture. "That's Birdie right?" he asked checking the image and then showing it to her. Snow nodded, not liking the way things were feeling.

Total fiddled with the phone, then held, it out in front of her and pressed a button.

An image of Birdie appeared on the screen and began moving. It showed him walk up to the door of a brownstone, but before his finger could touch the doorbell, the door opened wide and there stood Shawnee. Opening her arms she drew Birdie to her and rose up onto her toes. Snow didn't need a different view to be able to tell that they were kissing. When they broke the kiss, Birdie slipped pass Shawnee and entered the house. Shawnee stood for a dozen seconds checking up and down the block and then ducked back inside closing the door.

"You told me she was the one that called you most of the time before you shut down your phone right?" Total asked, moving the phone away then waving his hand at Chunky. Chunky came out of the hotel and came to the car. "Let the window down," Total said and Snow did it.

"Hit or miss?" Chunky asked, taking the phone Total held out.

"It's a hit...I'll call you in a few," Total replied and Chunky nodded, spinning around and making a dash to the hotel's door.

"You told him?" Snow asked staring at Total.

"Had to...we don't keep secrets Snow. He's ray people!"

"Shawnee's my family!"

"You still haven't answered my first question.... Was she the one that stayed on your caller I.D.?"

"Total?" Snow half-whined.

'"My father was family and he croaked my mother...he was family and I had a nigga stick a piece of steel in his chest. Was I supposed to leave you out here by yourself?"

Snow stared at Total, trying to grasp his revelation. He'd never volunteered to tell her anything about his escaping and she hadn't asked. Now he was telling her, that he'd had his own father killed, which meant it wasn't an accident that had happened and he'd taken advantage of being taken to the funeral. It had been planned from jump street.

"No," Snow whispered and dropped her head as she pulled on the fingers of her gloves just to have something to do. "No what?"

"No you weren't supposed to leave me out here by myself." Snow raised her head and Total saw the tears beginning to form in her eyes.

"She knew Ting-a-ling and Birdie did Drew and Alex...she knew you almost got killed by the same motherfuckers...she knew you had the crib down in Chelsea...she..."

"We grew up together, baby." The tears ran full force down her face. "She's family," Snow said sobbing and shaking. Total slid across the seat until he was up against her body and wrapped his arms protectively around her.

"Some things are thicker than blood Snow," he whispered, turning her face towards him. He kissed her forehead and then planted kisses along the trail of tears.

They sat holding each other for a good twenty minutes, before Snow pulled away and dug in her shoulder bag for a handkerchief. Total leaned back against the seat and watched silently as Snow cleaned up her face. When she was done, she turned to Total as she started the car. Leaning over, she kissed him.

"I love you man! Love you with everything that's in me and I always have…I do her," Snow said raising a gloved hand to his bearded chin and stroking it softly. If it comes down to it, you let me do it okay?" It was more of a plea than a question.

"If you think you can handle it."

"You handled your business…I'll handle mine," Snow said and pulled out into the street heading towards 6th Avenue.

"Wrong way to Brooklyn," Total said as Snow made a right.

"We ain't gong to Brooklyn."

"Where?"

"To meet some people," Snow replied flatly and made the turn to catch the parkway.

"It's kinda early for visiting ain't it?"

"Trust me…this time. They been waiting a long time to meet you, They won't mind one singe bit."

Chapter 18

"Come on sleepyhead!" Snow called as she shook Total's arm. Seeing he was awake, she climbed from the car and stretched in the rays of the sun coming up.

"I gotta take a piss," Total said turning to take in the unfamiliar surroundings.

"Tee inside!" Snow replied, coming around the car and taking him by the arm and leading the way towards a two-storied house. On the porch, Snow rang the single buzzer and it could be heard outside.

"I gotta go..." Total began, then stopped in mid-sentence as the door of the house swung open.

A tall, thin woman working to tie her robe over the long nightgown she was wearing stared at Total for all of a heartbeat and then her mouth fell open. She tried to cover it with her hand.

"Jasper?" she asked, then looked to Snow. Snow smiled and nodded her head. The woman stepped close to Total and wrapped her arms around his waist. "Thank the Lord," she moaned as she pressed her head against his chest.

Realization hit Total like a ton of bricks. He slowly wrapped his arms around his arms around the woman. Snow looked momentarily into his eyes and then turned pretending she was more interested in the rising sun, than what was going on between her man and the woman.

"Beverly?" Total asked, unwilling to believe that this was happening.

"Uh huh," she replied glancing up into his face.

Total's entire body shook and within seconds, tears were coursing down his cheeks and through his thick beard. They might have stood there forever, if two identical-looking boys hadn't stuck their heads out the door.

"What's wrong momma?" One ventured, his eyes glued to Total's as he watched them across his sister's shoulder.

"Nothing baby," Beverly replied loosening her grip, but hooking one arm around Total's waist. "Got somebody y'all need to meet... come out here."

The boys eased out of the doorway, but shied away from Total and drawing close to their mother.

"Who's he?" one of them asked. "Why you crying?"

"Because I'm happy...people do cry when they're happy," she explained rubbing the head of one and then the other. "You remember momma telling you about her brother?" Both boys nodded.

"The one they couldn't find," the shorter of the two volunteered, as he moved sideways and looked hard at Total.

"This is your uncle Jasper," Beverly said slipping away from Total and shoving him lightly towards them.

Total knelt down and held out his hand.

"Tell him your names!" their mother instructed.

"I'm Jamil," the taller one announced and reached out and took Total's hand. "He's Jasper like you, but he's shy!"

Total didn't realize he'd done it, till he was standing there with both of his nephews in his arms.

"Come on, we'd better get inside before we all freeze to death," Beverly said, pulling Total by his coat into the house. Snow followed, after sneaking an arm up to wipe her eyes.

It turned out, that Snow had been one very busy bee. She'd gone on-line and done a massive search. When the BCS had placed the rest of Total's brothers and sister, it had been under their real last names. Three years later they'd been given the names of the families that adopted them, since there wasn't any family that the system could find that were willing to take permanent custody of them. Total's brothers were living out in Ohio and Arizona. Beverly had lived in Levittown, Pennsylvania until she got married eight years before and then moved with her husband to Pittsburgh, with yet another name. But as it turned out, she'd been the easiest to find.

"You know we got the money you sent every month!" Beverly said as they sat around the kitchen table having finished breakfast. Before Total answered, he glanced towards Snow who was standing against one of the counters sipping coffee. She winked and gave him a short smile.

"I'm glad you did," Total replied, giving Snow a look that promised there was a long talk ahead.

"But why didn't you put a return address on the cards? His sister asked." We could have been in contact all these years.

"*Years?*" Total thought. He'd been figuring that this was something new.

"He moved around a lot Beverly...you can ask him about it later!" Snow interjected and looked towards the boys with her eyes. Beverly gave a slight nod of understanding and quickly switched the conversation.

"You know, I was hoping you two would be together. I used to watch Jasper watching you with those big moonstruck eyes," she said and the three grown up laughed.

Total and Snow spent most of the day at Beverly's. Before they left, Total had a short private talk with her. He told her every-thing but the circumstances of their father's death. No sooner were they out the driveway, than Total asked the question Snow knew instinctively would come.

"Why didn't you tell me?" he asked.

"Because I didn't think it would serve any real purpose. Bev had a life and kids to raise and you were in Elmira. It was hard enough on me, getting letters from you every week and not knowing if I'd ever see you out in the world again. The kids didn't need to know...don't need to know. That's why I always just sent a card and money...figured if I contacted her personally, there would be a whole lot of questions. You do understand?"

"Fo' sure," Total replied and scooped up Snow's hand. He didn't let go of it until they got back to Brooklyn, where Blaze and the Buffalo crew were waiting.

Chapter 19

"So what the fuck is going on?" the lieutenant demanded. "We got a war going on that nobody's caught wind of?"

"We don't think so lieutenant," Clay answered, looking up from where he'd been studying his hands to keep from having to look directly at the head of the homicide Division.

"Four bodies that point fingers at this Jefferies character, but nobody can place him even in the City and now two more homicides less than a dozen blocks away. Something's going on!

Clay looked at his partner Wash and Wash stood up, glanced around the lieutenant's office and spoke. "We've made the connection between Jefferies and the last two, but its shaky sir."

"Toss it out then...I'll decide." The lieutenant turned and look towards the wall filled with commendations.

Wash pulled out his memo book and fingered through it. He found what he wanted, but he waited until his boss was facing him. "We're theorizing, that Jasper Jefferies is cleaning house...the two crackheads...slash dealers were the brother and sister of the kid Jefferies killed when he was thirteen. The four bodies from 319 are supposedly in the employ... were I mean, supposedly working for a known drug dealer named Trench. Jefferies went down the last time, for killing two of Trench's people and he could have a beef. Somebody made the call to the Bronx stationhouse and told them what they feared might be happening."

The lieutenant stroked his chin, then sat down behind his desk. "Am I getting this right? Jefferies escapes from prison, comes back to the City with the intention to exact revenge on anybody he thinks or knows had done him wrong?"

"That's kinda our line of thought sir," Wash replied closing his memo book and sticking it back inside his jacket.

"So, the only thing we'd have to worry about is him killing anybody that fucked him around....No big deal huh?" Wash and Clay nodded in agreement. "Bullshit!" the lieutenant screamed and hit the padded top of his desk with the flat of his hand. "Sir..."

"You bet it's a big deal! Suppose he feels the D.A. that put him on trial fucked him? What about the judge? Or even the people that made up the Grand

Jury an indicted him? We're at mass murder numbers already! And it's no big deal?"

"Yes sir!" Wash replied. "When you look at it from your prospective. You're absolutely right, but we don't believe he's working on that scale." "He better not be!"

"Will you approve the extra men...to stakeout this guy Trench's drug spots?"

"You got any ideas about anyone else that might be on this guy's short list" The lieutenant opened his side drawer and took out a bottle of antacid tablets. He poured a half-dozen into his hand and tossed them into his mouth.

"Not yet, but we've got everybody and their mother looking for anything that points to him," Clay responded, his forehead crinkling as he watched the lieutenant chewing the tablets dry.

"I'm authorizing..." the lieutenant began and stopped, reaching for the silver pitcher of water that always sat on his desk and pouring himself a cup. Swallowing, he set the cup down and went on. "I'm authorizing you to pull anybody you need to get this done... I'll sign for the overtime!"

"Thanks lieutenant," Wash said, as he began moving Clay towards the office door.

"Just get it done, that'll be all the thanks I need!"

"Got you sir!" Wash said hustling Clay out of the office and down onto the first floor staircase.

"That sonofabitch, Clay hissed and glanced back

up the stairs.

"I second that, but we got what we wanted. Come on!" Wash said as two patrolmen started up the staircase.

"Trench is paying up, on top of those fucking Christmas bonuses and he's doing it tonight!" Clay growled.

"Call him!" Wash said pulling out a cell phone and giving it to Clay before walking around their car and climbing in behind the wheel.

"Fucking redneck motherfucker! Somebody should frag that fucker!" Clay said as he slid in next to Wash.

"Maybe we can find a way to get him on Total's list," Wash suggested starting and backing the car out into the street.

"Fucking real!" Clay said and spun his cap around backwards and leaned towards the dash. "Put the cracker on the list…and please don't miss…" Clay droned as he tapped the only beat out he knew against the dash.

Chapter 20

They entered the building one and two at a time. The first pair that went in took to the front and back staircases. They were the "*sweepers*," whose jobs was to make sure the staircases were clear of anything, or anybody that might be an obstruction or problem, when the rest of their crew was leaving the building. They'd also lead the way down when the time came.

On the landing of the floor above the one they wanted, they got rid of the lights by unscrewing and pocketing them. Almost simultaneously, they swept back their hooded sweatshirts and pulled on the Neoprene facemasks. The mask were black and covered everything, but their eyes. There were breather-holes across the mouth sections From beneath their coats, they pulled out nine-millimeters and attached the silencers.

Total and Chunky went directly to the elevators, upon entering the empty lobby. The one Chunky went to was already there, so he held it while Total pushed the call button for his and watched it slowly descend. By the time the elevator showed, the other three members of their crew were in the building and they loaded, up.

When the elevator Total was in stopped on five, he used the toe of his Engineer boot to hold the outside door open, while they pulled on their mask. Mask really weren't necessary, because it had been decided that nothing would be left alive when they left the apartment. There wouldn't be anything, or anyone to look at a line-up or photo array. The masks were to keep them from having to body everybody they ran into on their way out of the spot.

Murder came off the elevator first and moved directly to the heavy steel door of the apartment they wanted and went to work with his lock picks. It took less than two minutes for him to free the tumblers and pins so he could disengage the deadbolt. With an "*okay*" nod of his head, he spun away from the door dropping his picks into the cargo-pocket of his pants and pulling on his gloves. Chunky handed him one of the two silenced pistols he was holding.

Gun in hand, Total turned the doorknob and pushed the door as wide open as he could without it touching the wall behind it. Voices could be heard deeper in the apartment. Total went in and the rest followed, with Chunky taking up the rear. Pulling a half wooden wedge from his pocket, he closed the door and stuck it beneath it, then drew his second weapon and put his back to the door. Nobody would be coming through the door behind them.

Rushing the length of the hall, they separated with Total being responsible for the first room which happened to be the living room. A woman lay on her back, her jeans and panties hooked around one sneakered foot, while some nameless nigga with his pants down around his knees pounded away at her guts.

It took Total three long strides to reach the couch where the couple lay grunting and rolling against each other. He fired one shot for each step he took. The man's wide back took all three rounds.

"I know, you ain't finished already!" the woman half-shouted, as the man's body came down on her with all its lifeless weight. She raised her head just high enough to look over the man's shoulder at the sound of Total's boot hitting the coffee table and Total shot her through her left eye.

Total could hear the noises coming from the other areas in the apartment, but he paid them no attention until he was absolutely sure his two were dead.

The kitchen was the next room and Total found a woman wearing the bottoms of a fancy negligee crumpled by a sink filled with suds and dirty dishes. Pieces of her wig lay scattered, as the puddle of blood beneath her head grew bigger and bigger.

With the three bodies in the rear bedroom, there

had been a total of seven people in the apartment and Total hadn't recognized a single one of them.

His eyes on his watch and not on Chunky's people stuffing both drugs and money into a black nylon bag, Total pictured the way out the building. It was close to four in the morning, but a few late-night customers could appear.

"We're out!" Total shouted, after waiting for Murder to dump the last double-handful of money into the bag. Total was surprised, that they broke off and headed for the front' of the apartment, because from even where he stood he could see there was a lot more money in the desk drawer. Feeling even a deeper respect, Total followed them to the door where Chunky waited.

Putting one of his guns away, Chunky pulled free the wedge from beneath the door and swung it open. Murder went out first and they all followed, pulling the door closed. In the hall, they split up taking both sets of stairs.

*

At exactly five minutes after four, Snow started the engine of the van and shifted it into gear. She drove slowly up the block until she reached the building. She was just about to check her watch again, when the double doors of the building opened. They strolled to the van — heads down — two at a time. Snow reached back and slid the door open just as they reached the van. The first six climbed into the rear, while Total slid in next to her.

"Slow and easy baby, but get us out of here," Total said, then leaned forward below the dash to remove his mask and then pull up his hood so his face remained shadowed.

Snow drove the nine blocks, making sure to stay within the speed limit. When she pulled to the curb at 157th Street, Chunky and two of his people slipped out the van carrying the black nylon bag. Before one of the others slid the door closed, they had disappeared down into the subway.

Pulling off, Snow drove straight down 157th until she got to Amsterdam Avenue, where she made a right and drove until she hit 155th. Pulling over, she braked just long enough for the last three to climb out. The last one out was Murder and he dropped a red, nylon bag between the two Captain chairs where Snow and Total sat.

"Down the hill," Total reminded and motioned with his head. "The C or A-Train to Nostrand Avenue!" he added, reaching back and sliding the door closed. Murder nodded and crossed in front of the van.

"Which way honey?" Snow asked, pulling away.

"Take this to 125th, then head towards Riverside Drive," Total told her and slid the nylon bag from between the seats to the floor in front of him. Quickly opening the bag, he checked and found three guns and their silencers in it. Pulling his own weapon, he dropped it inside and pulled the bag's strings.

It took less than twenty minutes to reach their destination. Total had Snow pull the van beneath the overpass and park. They climbed from the van and Total passed Snow some keys and pointed to her Audi parked across the street.

"Start it...be right back!" Total called moving in the opposite direction, the bag in hand.

At the fenced railing that overlooked the river that separated New York from New Jersey, he glanced around to make sure there was nobody in the immediate area. Holding the bag in one hand, he spun around and launched it like a discus. It was too dark beneath the trestles to see the flight of the bag, but he heard it splash into the river.

The passenger side door was cracked when he got to the car. He slid in and Snow pulled away from the curb. "How'd my car get here?" Snow asked, glancing at Total as she made the turn to get up onto Riverside Drive proper.

"You know Blaze had to be doing something," Total replied and Snow giggled.

"Feeling naked again?" she asked. Total gave her a look that said it all. "Glove compart-ment...behind the first-aid kit."

Total popped the glove compartment and dug. His hand came out with the chromed 10mm pistol Max had shown him or their visit.

"How'd this get here?" he asked trying to recall when there would have been time for either Snow or Max to have made it happen.

"Max sent it...guess he needed to be doing something too," Snow replied, then reached to turn on the radio.

Chapter 21

Total had been hoping that the next shot they got at Birdie, would be one that would allow Shawnee to slip through the cracks, but it just wasn't to be. Gunz, the same one of Chunky's people that had gotten the pictures of Birdie swinging into Shawnee's crib, had taken an immediate interest and dislike to the nigga and had volunteered to continue shadowing him. Chunky had told Total that Shawnee looked just like one of Gunz's baby mamas and that he still had it bad for her, even though she wasn't parting with the pussy. When the call came, Blaze was on his way out the door to take care of some personal stuff, so Total didn't stopped him, even though he'd have prefer having him along.

When Total told Snow, she'd just gotten up from where she was beating the shit out of Chunky at Mercenaries 2 on the new Playstation 3 and went for her coat, gloves and bag. When Chunky had asked if there was anything he could do, Total had suggested that he pull Gunz in, because it was really personal. When they'd left for Harlem, Total was talking to Gunz on the phone.

When Total and Snow arrived at Shanee's place, Gunz was sitting on his gloves two stoops away. It was easy to tell by the icicles dangling from his moustache and the way he was shivering, that he'd been outside the whole time.

"You sure you don't need me to go in with you?" he asked standing and stomping his feet to get the circulation going.

"We're good. Thanks though," Total replied. They stood waiting until he got into one of the Impalas and drove away. "You say a credit card will get that door open?" Total asked, then watched as Snow dug in her bag and came out with one.

"She's always losing her keys...we got in more than a few times with one of these," Snow said flashing the card and moving up onto the porch. Total followed, keeping an eye out for anybody or anything that didn't look right.

"Bingo!" Snow whispered and pushed the door open.

"That easy upstairs?" Total asked closing and making sure the door was locked.

"Easier," Snow assured him and started up the steps on her toes. Total dug inside his coat and freed the 10mm Max had given him, At the top of the stairs, there were two doors. Snow moved to the rear one, then reached into her bag for the silenced 9mm. For a full minute, they stood listening for any sign of life. Total nodded.

Using the same credit card, Snow easily opened the door to the apartment and stepped aside. Easing the door open, Total found himself in the living room. There was one light on, on a small table. As they'd discussed, Snow closed the door and stood near it, as Total moved down the carpeted hallway to the bedroom.

Peeking into a bedroom lit by a dozen glass, scented candles, Total saw that both Birdie and Shawnee were asleep. Retracing his steps, he motioned for Snow to follow him. Near the door, he whispered his instructions. Sure she understood, he moved into the bedroom and to the side of the bed where Birdie lay snoring. Waiting until he was sure Snow was positioned he snatched the pillow from beneath Birdie's head and shoved it across his mouth as he pressed the gun against his forehead.

Birdie woke with a start. For a second he thought he was having one of his infrequent asthma attacks, because it was hard for him to breath, then he realized the pillow pressed against his lower face was the cause of the problem. He started to reach up to remove it but suddenly became aware of the cold steel pressed into the flesh of his forehead and the strange nigga doing the pressing.

"Shake her awake," Total said motioning to Shawnee. Birdie caught the arm that was flung out across his body and shook it.

"I'm tired Birdie!" Shawnee groaned and tried to free her arm, but Birdie didn't let it go and she was forced to open her eyes and look at him. "Shit no!" Shawnee shouted and slid backwards out of the bed butt-naked.

"You speak above a whisper and I make this about you, Total warned.

"I understand...no noise, just let me get my shit and get the fuck out of here," Shawnee said in an almost inaudible tone.

"Make it fast!"

Shawnee pulled on a pair of jeans, stuck her feet in a pair of furred boots and pulled a coat down that hung on the corner of the closet door.

"Real quiet baby...real quiet," Shawnee whispered pulling on the coat. "Can I take my bag?" she asked and motioned at a bag similar to the one Snow always carried laying on the floor. Total nodded. "I can get the fuck out of here?" she asked.

"Real quiet," Total told her and watched as she backed out of the room. "Now we talk," Total said speaking to Birdie, whose eyes seemed to have grown twice as large. "Where's the money and drugs you keep here?" Not yet! Just listen to the whole question," Total said as Birdie actually tried talking through the pillow. "When I take this pillow away, you're going to answer my question. You get one and only one shot to be straight-up with me, or..."

The sounds in the hallway outside the room, caused Total to break off. He distinctly heard the sound of the silenced pistol being fired once and then twice more, followed by the sound of something heavy hitting the floor. Birdie's eyes were on the door and before he could reshift them, Total shifted the pillow upwards and pressed the gun into it. He pulled the trigger twice. The gun made a loud noise, even through the pillow, but Total doubted it would carry far. The gun still jammed into the pillow, Total waited. A few seconds later, Snow stepped into the doorway.

"She could have walked...dumb, dick-sick bitch!" Snow muttered and glanced back into the corridor.

Lifting the pillow from Birdie's head, Total saw that the entire left hand side of his face was missing. Dropping the pillow, he moved to the doorway and saw Shawnee sprawled in the hall. Clutched in her hand, was a 32. Caliber semi-automatic. Bending over her, Total rolled her onto her back and saw the hole in her chin and another just above her left eyebrow.

"She could have had a walk Total," Snow repeated, as Total pulled the gun from her limp hand and laid his down on the carpet.

"We're out!"

Guiding her to the door with a hand at the middle of her back, Total checked the hallway and then motioned her down the staircase ahead of him. He kept the gun out, until they were exiting the outside door. Holding hands, they walked slowly to the far corner and climbed into the car parked there.

"Dumb bunny!" Snow spit and then went quiet, as Total crossed the intersection and headed towards lower Manhattan.

Chapter 22

It had been a long time since Blaze had played the late-night scene. For the past twelve years, he'd been living and laying low in Pennsylvania. An old body from back in the day had shown up when they tore down a building that he'd been part owner of. Enough rumors must have made it into the District Attorney's office, because he took it before the Grand Jury. It was all supposed to be secret, but Blaze had had enough clout, for a *"little birdie"* to whisper one word into his ear. The word was *"run"* and he'd done just that. Before he'd broken ground and sent the message to Total, nobody had known his whereabouts or even if he was alive. He'd sent a message to Total, that nobody but Total would be able to connect to him, and he'd done it, only because there was nothing but love in his heart for--now a man--the thirteen year-old he'd met so many years ago.

Blaze had been sitting in a cell at the precinct

waiting for the vans to show up to transfer him and the other adults in his pen to Central Booking. Some of the stupid niggas had tried to get rec at Total's expense. They'd called him every kind of faggot in the book, flashed their dicks at him and promised that the first time they got close to his pretty young ass that they were going to make him their woman. Total had stood unmoving at the bars of his pen and it was clear to an idiot, that he was putting faces to memory. After an hour, he waited until there were no police around and whispered a promise to kill any of them that he crossed paths with. It took a few minutes for the words that he had spoken so calmly to sink in and once they did, they got mad and began throwing wet toilet paper at him. When they'd, started harking up globs of spit to send his way, Blaze had waited until the first one spit and beat him unconscious with nothing but body shots. "That's my family...my nephew!" Blaze had declared and suddenly everybody involved was pretending that they'd been joking and their threats harmless. Before they could make Blaze come out his cell to be cuffed for the ride downtown, he'd made them give him a pen and piece of paper. He'd written down his address and two phone numbers that he could be reached at, after he made bail and had the police pass it to Total. Total had never called in the five years he'd spent at juvie, but he'd written twice. Once to ask for a pair of sneakers and again to ask what Blaze's birthday was. Four years in a row, he'd sent cards on or near Blaze's birthday without a return address or name. Blaze had been at Port Authority, the day they released Total and he'd been a part of his world since.

Giving the knock on the steel door—that he'd learned simply by watching other people going in--Blaze watched the slot in the door slide open. The doorman, like most of the people he'd seen going in, was new.

"Call McNasty!" Blaze shouted as the opening was reclosing. A couple minutes went by and the slot was opened again. Blaze immediately recognized the slitty eyes and bald, scarred head of the man who'd opened it.

"Motherfucker!" McNasty yelled, as he slammed the slot closed and went to work unbolting the door. "Where the fuck have you been you old bastard?" he added as the door swung open and he reached out and caught Blaze in a bear hug. He actually lifted Blaze off his feet.

Everybody in the immediate area, including the two security men with their shotguns, stood or sat still their eyes on the two figures in the door stunned. They were shocked, because the McNasty they knew, wasn't the type of nigga to give way to emotional scenes. Before he'd been nicknamed McNasty, he'd been Jesse McNaulty. He'd come to Harlem with nothing from somewhere in Alabama and once he'd gotten "*it*," he'd been willing to die to keep it. Two would be stickup men, had learned just how mean and nasty a nigga could get when you were taking something he'd worked long and hard to get. He'd beaten both of them to death with the leg off a table that had broken off, when they shot him and slammed him backwards into it. They'd given him thirty-five years and he'd done twenty-nine. The entire time he was in, he lifted weights, worked out religiously and read every book he could get his huge hands on. Because of his size and strength a lot of guards were intimidated by him, so he'd spent a lot of years in the box for what he called, *"Modifying ignorant behavior."* He'd come out of prison even meaner and nastier than he'd been before. Opening up yet another gambling spot, he'd installed a gym in the basement. He loved working out, but he cared more about making money and staying out of prison. There were only two rules--both displayed and verbally given. One, you didn't cheat and get caught in his place and two, no violence in the spot or anywhere in the block that surrounded it. Nobody was exempt and those that went against the rules, either had to undergo extensive physical therapy, or were never seen again. Rumor had it, that some of the people that had disappeared were buried beneath the cobblestoned basement floors. People that really knew McNasty though, knew that if the police ever showed up with picks and shovels, that all they would get out of it, was a good workout. McNasty wasn't dumb!

"If you'll put me down, I'll be able to breathe and I can tell you," Blaze replied and no sooner were his feet on the floor, than he was shooting two quick jabs at McNasty's middle.

"Still slow!" McNasty said, as he swept the punches away from his body with the edge of one hand. "Come on! My office!" he added as he slammed and threw the two inch-thick bolts on the door.

Polite...prison polite, McNasty didn't speak until after he'd poured two tumblers full of Johnnie Walker Blue and clipped the ends off some real Cuban cigars from his private stash.

"Must be important to bring you out of the woodwork," McNasty stated as he worked to get his cigar evenly lit.

"Kinda," Blaze replied as he dipped the end of his cigar into his glass, as he leaned onto the velvet-covered card table.

"Ain't no such thing as kinda Blaze."

"It is and it ain't."

"Use it in a sentence that makes sense and I'll go for it," McNasty challenged.

Blaze puffed away for a few, took a sip of the Johnnie Walker and looked up smiling with his eyes. I've got a twenty-two year-old girlfriend, that's kinda pregnant," he stated.

McNasty started coughing, as he tried to inhale the smoke from his cigar and laugh at the same time. Tears rolled down from his eyes as he bent almost double in his chair laughing and trying to suck in air. When the fit of laughter passed, McNasty just shook his head.

"Name it!" McNasty said, pulling his chair closer to the table and staring straight into Blaze's eyes.

"The Simmon brothers," Blazed replied lowering his voice.

"Lot of history and work in that!"

"It's all on me...just need to know if you've got a problem with it." Unlike most fools, Blaze knew where the real strength rested in Harlem. McNasty may not have his hand stuck out to collect a dime on every dollar made in Harlem, but he "was" one of the niggas whose will people bent to...whose position they respected.

"We go back quite a few years...me and those Simmon boys," McNasty offered opening the door for explanations.   "Their boss crossed my nephew. They knew it and they still take paper from him."

"Total-E?" McNasty asked and Blaze nodded. "Then we might say that the possibility exist, that he's in the City and may be the cause of Trench's new headache."

"That's a good possibility."

"How long have we known each other Blaze?"

Blaze thought for a few seconds then responded. "Ten years before you got out the prison."

"Been a long time. Guess I don't have to tell you

my answer then?"

"Nope...that's deniability," Blaze said and stuck out his hand. McNasty took it, set aside his glass and worked his way around the table. He hugged Blaze yet again.

"They still come through most nights as usual... sure you don't need a hand before I forget how?" he whispered near Blaze's ear.

"I'm good Jesse...not taking any chances. You keep doing what you do so well," Blaze replied his mouth near McNasty's ear, where there wouldn't be a doubt about the possibility of their having been overheard.

"You stay safe." McNasty broke the hug and slipped one arm around Blaze's massive shoulders, as the walked toward the door leading back into the club.

❦

Three nights after his talk with McNasty, Blaze watched the Simmon brothers climb out of a brand new convertible BMW and stroll into the hallway of the building. He made a quick phone call and let the car seat back so he could stretch out. Thirty minutes later, a Taxi pulled up on the opposite side of the street and he watched a young girl climb out and pay the driver. She stayed on the side of the street she'd gotten out on, until she glanced back and saw the taxi was out of the block. Crossing, she moved down the block stopping on the passenger side of Blaze's Caddy. Blaze hit the lock.

"This better be good Blaze...got me dressing up like some juvenile delinquent hooker...in this cold!" the girl said, slamming the door closed and leaning over to give Blaze a kiss on his stubble chin.

"Missed you too," Blaze replied, looking her over. "How old are you now?!! he asked and dropped his huge paw onto the girl's uncovered thigh.

"Thirty-six."

"And you still look fourteen. Damn!"

"That's why you called me right?"

"Yeah, but not for me."

"Nigga I know that! You ain't gotta tell me, 'cause if you'd wanted it...you could've had it when I was seventeen. So, who's the vick?"

"The Simmon brothers," Blaze replied, his eyes never leaving the doorway of the building for more than a few seconds.

"Them negroes...shit, I'll work for free. They ain't shit! pedophile-assed motherfuckers!"

"It's a done-dah-dah Bebe."

"For free, but you gotta give me your word on something...you know I don't ask much of you, 'cause you've always been there for me no matter what."

"I'm listening Bebe."

"You gotta tell them it was me that set 'em up... probably forgot me...wouldn't recognize me now, but they got to know. You just say Trinidad's daughter... they'll remember. Okay?"

Blaze sat silent for a minute, his eyes leaving the doorway as he tried to encompass the hate and pain that was reflected in Bebe's eyes. He'd known her since she was a kid and though she'd talked to him about a lot of her rough life, she had never revealed or even hinted at the possibilities of her having been one of the Simmon brother's victims and she'd been around them a lot of years. If Blaze had even guessed, he wouldn't have to be here tonight and she wouldn't be bait.

Blaze took several deep breaths, glanced across the street and then back at Bebe. "You've got my word on it!" he stated and turned his head so he wouldn't see anymore of the pain in her eyes.

"*Mother...fuckers!*" Blaze thought, trying to keep his anger from surfacing. He knew, that when you acted in anger, you could make a mistake and he wasn't feeling like making one tonight.

Chapter 23

"I'm getting tired of this shit Clay!" Wash said glancing back across the street where Ting-a-ling stood staring at them from behind his Detiali. "I should go slap that bitch-ass nigga in his motherfucking mouth!"

"What the fuck is it going to prove? Besides it still ain't gonna keep you from being pulled out of the bed before daybreak!" Clay said.

"Nigga's packing heat...could run him in...let him sit in the bullpens half the day."

"You forgetting that's Ace Lake's only son now? He'd be out no sooner than the old man got the call." Clay unlocked the SUV and reached in to unlock the passenger side.

"I'm not feeling this shit. I think Trench is lying to us!"

"You think Ace and him are hooked up some-how?"

"How else would he know Ace has got money

out for Jefferies?"

"Same way we hear things," Clay said starting the engine. "The streets talk."

"Then why we ain't hear nothing about it? We got a dozen sets of ears glued to the pavement and ain't nobody even hinted Ace is looking for that motherfucker!"

"Wash?"

"Yeah?"

"You heading for a major stroke. Stop trying to figure every little thing out. We hit Trench in the head for an extra ten-big and it ain't even Christmas yet."

"He owed us that."

"Yeah, but he gave us another bonus," Clay said staring across the street to where Ting-a-ling and one of his henchmen were trailing behind the gurney being wheeled towards the yawning door of the meat wagon.

"I'm not catching that."

"He proved we were right...that nigga is after anybody that crossed him. You don't just put money "like that out trying to be a good Samaritan... somebody in that crew did something to our boy," Clay said pulling away from the curb.

"Our boy?"

"Long as he keeps Trench scared enough to pass off like he's doing."

Chapter 24

Slipping her cell phone into her pocket, Bebe left the warmth of the hallway. Glancing down along the empty block, she watched the two men come out the distant building and head for their car. Waiting until they car's lights lit up half the block, she walked a dozen feet and stepped off the curb between a stripped Mercury Cougar and an almost new Nissan Maxima. Slipping her hands beneath her short skirt, she caught the waistband of her panties and waited, when the car was thirty feet away, she snatched down her panties and squatted. Straining, she got the pee to flow. When she knew the car was close enough for the occupants to have seen her fine, red ass, she stared at the car like a deer caught in a hunter's headlights and then quickly stood snatching up her panties and began walking away.

Stepping up onto the sidewalk, Bebe walked to the corner. As the light changed, she crossed a 110th

Street and was almost up on the opposite sidewalk when the car's horn sounded and the BMW cruised by her and entered the block. Glancing towards the car, she stretched her already big eyes trying to look panicked and began walking as fast as she could. In truth, the wind was an incentive as its cold breeze whipped around her legs and beneath the skirt. The car's occupants blew the horn twice, but Bebe didn't stop walking until she was in the block between 108th and 107th.

She watched the car until the window rolled down, then stepped off the curb. "*You're half-scared*" she reminded herself and stopped a good six feet away.

"What do you want?" she asked timidly, as she bent to see pass the driver to take in the other occupant.

"Little party," the driver said and hung his fingers outside the car, a hundred-dollar bill between them.

"Please tell me you guys aren't cops?" Bebe pleaded. Laughter floated from the car.

"We definitely ain't the po...lice! How old are you honey?" The driver called to her, as he lifted the shades from his reddened eyes so he could get a good look at her.

"Fif...seventeen, almost eighteen," Bebe replied. The crooked smile on the man's lips said he'd caught what she'd purposely began to say.

"You wanna make some quick money or what?" he asked again as he added another bill to the one he'd flashed and begin tapping the side of the car with them.

"My momma told me not to go in anybody's car... even if I knew 'em."

The driver bent towards his passenger, then looked back. "You live around here?"

"Next corner 107th," Bebe said motioning with her hands. "My momma got locked up...we can go there...not doing nothin' till I get the money though." she stuck her hands and in her pockets and began shifting from foot to foot like she was cold.

"Up or down the hill?"

'"Up, almost on Amsterdam." she watched the car pull off and make the turn, she crossed the street and trailed after it.

By the time Bebe turned into the block, the two men were outside the car and waiting on her. She smiled as she drew close and dropped her head shyly.

"Come on," she called walking pass them and onto the porch of the building two doors away.

"You actually live in this?" one of them asked as they followed her up the stairs to the second floor. She ignored the question.

Stopping at the second door on the floor, she pulled out a key and jammed it into the lock. She pretended she was having trouble with it, then giggled and unlocked the door. She smiled to herself, because anybody with a key--any kind of key--could unlock the stripped out door. Pushing the door open, she stepped aside and let them enter the lit hallway.

Closing and then locking and chaining the door, she walked pass them and into the bright bedroom.

"Can I have the money please?" she thought about their slimy hands and it reflected on her face. She looked very uncomfortable.

"No sheets baby?" the man asked as he fished the two bills from his pocket and held them out to her.

"Sure...momma says to always use clean sheets," Bebe replied and moved to the closed closet door swinging it wide open. The only things in the closet were an old woman's leather coat and a shelf filled with sheets and towels.

Reaching up onto the shelf, Bebe took down a set of sheets and a handful of towels with different hotel names on them. Spinning around, as she felt one of them moving close to her, she tossed everything on the bed.

"Get comfortable!" she told them as she pulled off her fake fur and let it drop to the floor. Their bulging eyes said they were impressed with her firm, thick-nippled breast that were visible through the sheer material of the tiny halter top she had on. "I've got to finish my pee-pee," she added as girlishly as she could manage and turned to go out the room.

"I get her first!"

"You always go first Bert...this young bitch is prime! First one naked, get's to break her in *right*"! The other man said and began pulling off his coat.

While Bert was pulling off his coat, he toed off his

turtle-skinned shoes to catch up. They were both down to their boxers, when Blaze eased the leather coat in the closet aside and stepped out with a huge, .357 Colt Python in his hand. The other man saw him first.

"Blaze?"

"Guess you ain't that old Satch!" Blaze replied and Bert turned his hands at the waistband of his underwear.

Blaze saw Bebe quick-step pass the room heading for the door.

"What the fuck is this Blaze?" Bert demanded looking stupid as hell with garters fastened around his skinny calves to hold up his silk socks.

"Just shut the fuck up Bert...all you do is run your fucking mouth!" Blaze said as his brain flashed across quite a few incidents that had brought him into contact with the brothers. He hadn't liked them then and he really didn't like them now.

"You rob us...you got serious beef!" Satch stated.

"Yeah Blaze, you ain't lived this long by doing stupid shit," Bert tossed in as he glanced to where the rest of his clothes lay in a pile, wondering if he could drop and roll and get to the clip-on holster with his .38 in it.

"You niggers really don't understand, do you? You didn't even recognize the girl....Just how foul are you niggers living?" Blaze cocked the hammer back on the gun.

"Hold Blaze!" Satch raised his hands and looked

at his brother. "If she's yours, our bad man!"

"You remember Trinny...Trinidad with the pretty green eyes?"

"Shit yeah! Who the fuck wouldn't remember her Blaze?" Bert asked.

"Then why the fuck don't you remember her kid?" Blaze asked and the brothers' eyes got big at the same time. "This is for her!" Blaze growled and pulled the trigger. It looked like a foot of flame came from the gun's barrel, lifted Satch Simmon up from the floor and slammed him into the wall a dozen feet away.

When Blaze shifted his aim to tap Bert, Bert had already gone to the floor and had reached the pile of clothes. Bert didn't even bother trying to free the gun from the holster, he just aimed and fired. He fired at the same instant Blaze did.

"Fuck!" Blaze roared, as his left leg was slammed from beneath him and he went straight down. It was the only thing that saved his life, because if he'd remained in that same space, Bert's second shot would have done him. Catching himself on one hand, he fired at Bert three times. The first shot slid Bert backwards on one hip. The second and third promised that he wouldn't have an open casket at the funeral.

"Shit.,.shit...shit!" Bebe screamed as she peeked into the room and saw Blaze down. "We got to get you out of here Poppa Bear!" Dropping down into a crouch, Bebe slipped her shoulder up under Blaze's armpit. Catching a chunk of his coat, she used every ounce of strength she had to stand up. Blaze came up with her.

On his feet, Blaze shifted most of his bodyweight to his right leg and using Bebe as a crutch, he hobbled to the open door of the apartment. The going was easier on the stairs, with Bebe on one side of him and the banister on the other, but by the time they hit the street Blaze was breathing hard.

"The car baby...where's the car?" Bebe asked.

"Just pass the lot!" Blaze replied and pointed towards the corner across the street. He was moving before she did, almost running as he gritted his teeth.

"Where to?" Bebe asked, shoving Blaze into the car and running around to climb behind the wheel.

"Anywhere...anywhere at all!" Blaze groaned, as he dug through the glove compartment and started pulling out rags that he used to clean and wax the car.

"You need a hospital," Bebe said, glancing at him as she burnt rubber coming away from the curb.

"Anywhere, but a hospital," he replied grimacing as he pressed the padded-up rags against the entrance wound in his thigh.

"My fucking fault! Fuck! Fuck! Fuck!" Bebe shouted out loud as she spun the wheel and headed in the direction of Central Park.

"This is on me baby...let myself get mad for the first time since I was a kid," Blaze said trying to assure her.

"Yeah, but you got mad behind me," she whined.

Chapter 25

"Weed Mon?" Total called from the doorway, adopting the Jamaican accent he'd mastered to go along with him being listed as a Rastafarian, which was the only way he was allowed to grow his dreads. "Got some fo' ya Mon!" he added making his dreads dance around his shoulders, as he pulled a baggy filled with Haze from the pocket of his Army coat.

Ace relaxed. *"Fucking dreadnaught"* he thought and took a step, releasing his grip on the gun in his overcoat pocket.

"Nah wan' regularrrrr...got dah 'dro Mon!" Total called pulling his other hand from his pocket, as Ace looked back. "Or maybe you be needing some of this!" Total snarled and pointed a .38 semi-auto at Ace as he came down the steps.

"What the fuck!" Ace exclaimed taking several steps sideways to put some space between him and whoever the fuck it was.

"Don't even think it!" Snow whispered, stepping up onto the sidewalk from behind the van, where she'd been hiding and pressing the barrel of the silenced 9mm flush against Ace's temple.

"I got him now," Total said, as he dipped a hand into Ace's coat pocket and retrieved the gun it held. "You go get the car...I get the money and we're out of here!"

"I got you babe!" Snow replied and headed up the block, after sticking the gun into her shoulder bag.

"Move Ace! Inside!" Total ordered, shoving the gun hard into Ace's kidney. Ace grunted and moved up the stairs to the door of his brownstone. When Ace fumbled with the keys, Total slammed him face first into the ornate steel gate that protected the wooden door behind it. "Don't fuck with me!"

"I got it Total...got it," Ace whimpered, a hand to his bloody lips. He'd thought it was Total, but wasn't sure till he saw Snow.

Shoving Ace into the corridor, Total flipped the lock on the closed door and ordered Ace up the stairs, where he'd been told the safe was.

"You got three minutes to show me the money, or you get buried with your son," Total said coldly. Ace lead the way to a modified den and shoved the Chinese screen aside that hid part of one wall.

The safe stood almost six-foot high. It wasn't one of the cheap ones; it had been made to withstand almost anything. The phone in Total's pocket vibrated once and then quit, which meant Chunky and his people had taken Ace's right and left hands out of the game.

"Open it!" Total said, pulling back the hammer on the gun he'd taken from Ace. Ace knelt, started fiddling with the huge dial and then stopped and turned to look up at Total.

"You're going to kill me anyway man." there was a slight tremor in his voice. He swallowed.

"Look nigga, all I want is the money and I'm out...you don't open it and I'm doing you. That's a fact," Total warned.

"I've known you since you were a kid and all you do is croak niggers. You want me to believe, that you're not going to do me?" Total nodded his head slowly. "Then give me your word...I know you don't break your word! Give it to me and I open the safe and there's at least a quarter of a million in it...it'll be yours."

Total stood staring at Ace. Ace had always been a thinker, that was why he couldn't understand why he'd allowed his sons to go at Alex and Drew, Snow's brothers. He could understand him having gotten rid of Snow's father, but not coming at Snow.

"Did you have Vick done?" Total asked.

"Gimme your word. I tell you the truth and open the safe."

Total glanced at his watch, the three minutes he'd promised were up.

"You open the safe and make me believe that you're telling the truth about Vick...on everything I love...my word, I won't kill you! Nothing else to talk about!"

Ace turned back to the safe, spun the dial to three different numbers and then turned the handle swinging the safe door open. "You got it," Ace said standing and backing away so Total could see the rows upon rows of banded money stacked almost to the top of the top two sections of the safe.

"Vick?"

"I did him personally...we was partners, but we didn't have the same visions. He wanted to pull out and go legit, but he'd been in the game long enough to stack where he could do that. I did it, 'cause I couldn't let some dumb nut do somebody that was like family to me," Ace explained, his hands and double chin visibly shaking. "You gave your word!" Ace added as he watched Total drop his head and begin mumbling beneath his breath.

"But I didn't!" Snow screamed and waited until Ace spun towards her voice to fire.

"Snow no!" Ace howled even as the first shot blew away his kneecap and sent him crumpling to the floor. "I loved you...like a daughter...damn Snow!" Ace cried as he held his shattered knee with both hands.

"Like a daughter?" Snow asked cocking her head in disbelief and firing another silenced 9mm round that didn't hit what she'd aimed at, but blew off one of Ace's fingers. "You motherfucker!" Snow cried as tears began rolling down her smooth cheeks. That was when she lost it, emptying the remainder of the fifteen-round clip into Ace's face, neck and head.

When the gun cocked back empty, Snow harked to spit and would have if Total's gloved hand hadn't attached itself to her face. She stared at him wide-eyed.

"DNA baby...DNA," Total whispered against the side of her neck as he pulled the gun from her hands and wrapped his arms around her body to pull her back against him. "You handled your business baby... it's cool. Trust me!" Pulling out his phone, he pressed the six and listened to it ring.

"Yo dog?" Chunky answered.

"Got a crackhead soup for you...come get it!" Total replied and snapped the phone closed.

Total was still holding Snow, when he heard the feet pounding up the stairs. He shifted so he could see the doorway, relaxing and lowering his gun only when he saw Chunky's face.

"Motherfucker dog! Fucking Bingo!" Chunky said as he caught sight of the money stacked in the safe. "Find something to put this paper in!" he shouted as Gunz and one of his other people came through the door. They spun around and returned moments later with a pillowcase and a Gucci carryon.

"Your other people okay?" Total asked, watching them shift the money into the bag and pillowcase.

"They'll be at the house when we get back. They're dropping off that dirty laundry," Chunky said, then reached deep into the safe and came out with a huge gold chain, a diamond pendant dangling from it. Snow stared at it, almost as if she was hypnotized.

"I need that," Total said looking at Snow and then back at Chunky. "I'll pay for it."

Chunky jangled the chain and moved over to where Total and Snow stood. "On me," he replied and held it out to Snow. Snow's hand shook as she took it and then pressed it against her chest with both hands.

"DNA," Total breathed and used one of his gloved hands to wipe at the tears coming down Snow's face.

Chapter 26

"Hello?" Snow asked, having picked up Total's phone from between them on the car's eat. "You're calling for who?" Snow demanded, listened and then handed Total the phone.

"Yeah? Yeah I'm his nephew....Where's he at?" Total listened and then snapped the phone closed and dropped it back onto the seat.

"What's wrong baby? She called Blaze Poppa Bear," Snow said, suddenly getting an uneasy feeling.

"Blaze got shot. That was Bebe, he's at her crib over on Park Avenue," Total told her.

Snow remained silent, fingering the chain in her coat pocket. She could see it in Total's eyes, though each of his movements as he drove was controlled. It took them twenty-five minutes to get to Park and 57th and then another ten minutes to find somewhere to park the car.

The building's doorman met them and after

calling up to make sure they were expected, he buzzed them into the lobby. Snow held Total's hand during the elevator ride, but still hadn't uttered a single word since he'd told her what had happened. She knew that, there was nothing she could say, that would make it any better. From experience, she knew that where he could talk to her and make things seem better, the opposite occurred when she tried to make it work for him.

Bebe opened the door before the echo of the buzzer died and led them into the bedroom. Blaze lay in the center of a huge, pink canopied bed. He lay on his back snoring, wearing a foot-wide swath of padded gauze around his left thigh.

"Doc gave him something for the pain...so he could sleep," Bebe explained as Total and Snow stood over him.

"A doctor?" Total asked.

"One of my clients...I'm not stupid Total," Bebe replied softly and then turned and looked at Snow. "How you been Aljiva? Ain't seen you in years."

"Chillin' Bebe....Why didn't you just say your name girl?" Snow said and giggled. "Had me thinking all kinds of crazy shit especially you calling him Poppa Bear!"

"He's that...come on, it'll probably be awhile before he wakes up hungry." Bebe turned and walked out of the room with Snow and Total following. "Got coffee and turnovers!" Bebe offered as they entered a kitchen that was almost as big as the bedroom, they'd just left. Ducking beneath the counter, Bebe came up in the center of the kitchen island.

"Both!" Total replied.

"Just coffee Bebe, I'm trying to watch my weight," Snow replied and climbed up onto one of the high back chairs. Bebe laughed and picked up a silver, coffee server. "A bitch should have to worry as hard as you do," she said and slid a cup over and filled it with what Snow could smell was *"real"* coffee.

Total just shook his head at the interchange. They'd all known each other most of their lives, having grown up in the same area. There had been a time, when Total had, had eyes for Bebe but the kind of paper chase she'd been on since she was like fifteen had killed it. She'd been hooking since she was fourteen. Like Snow, she'd been tall for her age, but anybody that looked at her, no matter how much makeup she put on to look older, knew that she was a kid. But she hadn't changed a bit in over seventeen years.

"So, he tell you what went down?" Total asked, stirring creamer and three heaping spoons of sugar into his coffee between bites of an apple turnover, that was too big and too full of apples to have come from anywhere but a seriously expensive bakery.

"I was with him...told me not to talk to anybody but you and Snow," Bebe explained slipping from inside the island and climbing up onto the seat at the counter where her own cup was at. Taking a sip of her coffee, she told them what had happened and Total listened intently. When she'd finished, both of the women found themselves looking at Total, who was sitting with his head down.

Feeling the eyes on him, Total looked up. "He did it for me," he confessed. "Should have known he was up to something, when he kept disappearing from the house. Damn!"

"You can't blame yourself alone...! gotta take part of that weight," Bebe said, but didn't expound on it and neither Snow or Total pushed.

An hour and a half later, Blaze woke hungry as Bebe had predicted. They all stood around and watched him wolf down a dozen eggs, toast, bagels and two apple turnovers. Bert's bullet had missed anything vital, passing through flesh and muscle and then exiting. Doc had predicted a couple weeks to heal and maybe a month or two of physical therapy to get him "*almost*" back to normal.

When Blaze asked what had been going on, Bebe found a reason to leave the room and Total took him through it. Snow had allowed Blaze to hold the chain and it seemed to do a lot of good for him, even though he admitted that he hadn't known that Snow's father had intended to get out of the business. They'd stayed until late afternoon, said their goodbyes and headed back to Brooklyn.

Chapter 27

"So what's the word dog?" Chunky asked, looking pass Total to where his crew lounged in the twin Impalas, the engines running.

"Buffalo my nigga!" Total answered smiling, even though he was already yearning the loss of company that he could relate to. It was fucked up, but after being locked up almost a decade, he hadn't been able to find anything in common with the regular people he'd met on the streets. It was like either he, or they were from another planet.

"I don't know if I'm feeling it dog...still got some business to handle. That's why I rolled."

"What's left on one side ain't shit...fucking Ting-a-ling. The other side is strictly personal, like I hipped you to from the door," Total explained.

"That nigga could turn out to be a problem."

"Trust me Chunky, he won't even see it coming," Total said lying for the first time ever to his man, because his intentions were to be looking Ting-a-ling in his eyes when he put him down.

"We'll be rolling back through here for New Years you know?"

"Then set it off for me...don't intend to be anywhere on the East coast if I can help it," Total said smiling, but wondering if not being able to be a part of the normal world, was why Chunky swung with a crew made up of niggas that had done bids.

"You know you could hang out with us, up our way." Chunky winked. Total laughed at the thought.

"Naw dog, y'all too rowdy for my taste. Besides, Snow wants to see what the West coast is like."

"Hang below the radar wherever you be. Don't know if I'll be able to pry yo' ass loose again if something happened," Chunky said, the cheerfulness gone from his tone.

"Bet!" Total stepped close and hugged Chunky to him. They pounded each other's backs and then broke apart.

"Shit "*almost*," got as real as the "burn," Chunky said almost as an afterthought as he spun and started walking away.

"*Almost*" Total thought, not wanting to stretch the goodbyes out any longer. It was getting hard. At the car, Chunky turned and held both hands up shoulder-high.

"You sure you don't need none of that paper dog?"

"It was never about the paper Chunky...we're good," Total told him and with a shrug of his shoulders, Chunky strolled around the front of the first car and climbed into the car with Murder and Gunz.

Total stayed where he stood until both rocking cars had pulled out the driveway and made the turn at the corner.

❧

"Pull over Murder!" Chunky said less than two blocks from the house.

"What? Man I knew it!" Murder said easing the car to the side of the block and glancing in the rearview mirror to be sure the second car was following his example.

"You called it Murder!" Gunz said from the backseat.

"You staying ain't you?" Murder asked, as Chunky opened the door and slid his legs out.

"Pop the trunk!" Chunky said not bothering to answer and climbed out closing the door behind him.

The trunk opened and Chunky reached inside and pulled out the plastic-wrapped leather coat with the mink collar he'd been wearing when they first met Total at Shadows. Ripping the plastic off, he folded the coat and slung it over one shoulder. Reclosing the trunk, he walked around to the driver's side of the car and leaned onto the open window.

"You that nigga till I get back....Feel me dog?" Chunky asked Murder, while looking back towards the other car.

"You know we'll all ride with you!" Murder voiced.

"Ain't about y'all dog...y'all come thru like always and I already know. This is about me and my homie, that ain't a homie. You feel me?"

"Got that!" Murder replied.

"I'll give them the what's up and y'all be out," Chunky said motioning with a nod of his head. Reaching into the car with a gloved hand, he made a fist and both Gunz and Murder tapped it with their own. Turning to walk away, Chunky stopped and looked back. "That's a direct dog!" he added and then strolled down the block to the other car.

Chunky spoke to his people for a couple, or three minutes and then stepped up onto the curb and watched both cars pull off. When they were specks a dozen blocks away, he pulled the leather coat from his shoulder and put it on.

Ringing the bell, Chunky watched Snow appear and head to the door. She pulled it open, then looked out it, looking for the cars. Taking a step back she called Total's name.

"Thank you," Snow whispered, as Total's footsteps could be heard coming down the steps. Chunky smiled and gave her a wink.

"That's what real dogs do," he muttered.

"What's up babe?" Total asked and Snow stepped aside and away from the door so he could see pass her.

"Aw man! What the fuck are you doing? You're supposed to be halfway to Buffalo!" Total said at the sight of Chunky.

Shrugging his shoulders, Chunky walked pass Total and into the house. Slouching down onto the sofa, he picked up one of the controls for the Gameboy. "Forgot to say my goodbyes to the triple-O.G.," he said glancing up at Total and then motioned with the control in his hand at Snow. She came over and picked up the other control.

"He's Uptown, I'll give you the address!" Total said, already knowing he was beating a dead horse.

"Write it down...know how my memory is and soon as I take care of some "*unfinished*" business, I'll handle it." Chunky turned and looked at Snow. "Forget the Mercenary stuff Snow...you wanna be the big dog, you gotta do Chunky at N.B.A. man!"

Trying not to smile, Snow sat down her control and went over to the box below the flat-screened monitor and pulled out the N.B.A. cartridge. Ejecting the cartridge in the Play Station, she moved back over to the sofa and sat down.

Tossing up his hands in defeat, Total headed back towards the kitchen. "I got winners!" he called back and Snow had to cover her mouth with her hands to keep him from hearing her laughing.

Chapter 28

For three days in a row, Ting-a-ling had tried and couldn't connect with his father, or any of his crew. A check of the three spots they still had up and working produced the same results. Nobody had seen, or heard from Ace since the night before when Birdie had been murdered. On the day of Birdie's funeral, with Chi-low and Flow in tow, he'd gone to his father's house. He rang the bell and pounded on the door through a space in the steel security gate, until the neighbors began peeking out their windows or coming outside to investigate.

"Come on Ting, for somebody call the police... he'll show up at the funeral, you know he wouldn't miss that!" Chi-low said pulling Ting-a-ling by his suited arm.

"Might be with your other family," Flow suggested as they climbed into the rented black Suburban.

"Other family?" Ting-a-ling asked, staring at Flow over the car seat.

"Yeah, the ones that was supposed to come in Sunday night! Them St. Louis people yo' pops always be rapping about!" Flow said.

Two wrinkles suddenly appeared in Ting-a-ling's forehead and he pounded the steering wheel with the heel of his hand. "How the fuck did I forget about that! That was three days ago, right when Pop stopped answering his phone," Ting-a-ling said and looked at Chi-low as he started the truck.

"Said you didn't trust them niggas anyway," Chi-low reminded him.

"We gonna check on that shit! Right after the funeral, especially if Pop don't show up!"

"You thinking what I'm thinking?" Chi-low asked waving to one of the neighbors that was standing in her doorway watching them.

"That we might be giving credit to the wrong motherfuckers?" Ting-a-ling asked pulling out of the parking space. Chi-low gave him a short nod, then dug in his pocket and pulled out a sack of weed and tossed it to Flow in the backseat.

"Them motherfuckers!" Ting-a-ling screamed as he came out of the church.

"Just chill Ting," Chi-low said in a low voice as he tried to move Ting-a-ling off the steps of the church and towards the parked Suburban.

"Twenty-nine lousy niggas show up to put my

baby brother in the ground? That's cold disrespect! We be letting those niggas stack paper and instead of showing up to even fake like they going to miss a nigga...they out here slinging!"

"Chill Ting...police and they listening hard," Chi-low said and turned Ting-a-ling around so he could see the cops he'd been referring to.

"Fuck the police!" Ting-a-ling roared and skipped around the front of the truck and climbed in.

"We going to the cemetery right?" Chi-low asked as soon as he was inside.

"Hell no! We got two things to do...teach those niggas some respect and find out where the fuck my Pop's at! Ain't nothing else coming before that!

"You sure they ain't still on us?" Ting-a-ling asked, continuing to check the rear and side mirrors.

"Not since 72nd," Chi-low answered, dipping his head and taking a pull on the joint Flow had passed him.

"Then let's be there!" Ting-a-ling said and turned to head back toward the West side of Harlem.

They passed the joint around until they reached 8th Avenue, where Ting-a-ling cruised to stop just before he reached the intersecting street.

"We doing a warning or what?" Chi-low asked, as he transferred his Clock from the paper bag it had been in, into his overcoat pocket.

"We dressed for a funeral right?" Ting-a-ling

asked.

"Enough said," Chi-low replied and climbed out of the car.

"Why you sitting there Flow?" Ting-a-ling demanded, after not hearing the rear door open and looking back.

"Thought you wanted me to hang with you," Flow told him.

"Nigga...swear you don't get the fuck out this car..." Ting-a-ling began, but didn't get to finish, as Flow shoved the door wide and jumped out. He slammed the door so hard, Ting-a-ling jumped. "Bitch-assed nigga!"

Counting to fifty, Ting-a-ling pulled the truck to and around the corner into the block. By the time he passed the stoop where the niggas that should have been at Birdie's funeral were working off of, Flow had caught up with Chi-low. Stopping and double parking thirty feet from the building, Ting-a-ling climbed from the truck and began walking at an angle through the street.

"Yo...yo niggas!" Ting-a-ling called as he neared the stoop still in the street and a position that allowed the car parked there to hide the gun in his hand. "Y'all diss my brother to sell crack?" Everybody on the stoop was looking towards Ting-a-ling, now that they realized who and what the yelling was about. They never saw Chi-low and Flow raise their guns and squeeze off.

Ting-a-ling smiled ugly and stepped up onto the sidewalk and fired four shots of his own, into the yelling, screaming, bloody mess. Seeing Chi-low and Flow break, he turned and ran after them.

"What it look like?" Ting-a-ling asked, as he sped down the length of the block at 60-mph one hand fucking with the radio.

"Anybody that was out is gone...clear on this side!" Chi-low called as he knelt on the backseat watching the sidewalk and building doors.

"Like a ghost town," Flow chimed in and then spent around and slumped down onto the car seat as a case of the giggles from the Haze rolled through him.

Chapter 29

"Nigga's wilding out, if you ask me," Chunky said sliding into the car and slamming the door. "Better roll dog, it's hotter than Spring break in South Beach "round here!"

"Who?" Total asked starting the car, but keeping an eye on the crowd of people gathered at the barricade the police had erected to keep cars from entering.

"Yo boy Ting-a-ling, is now Ding-a-ling!"

"You jiving?" Total stated as he dipped in between two cars and began driving Uptown. His question was purely reflex, because he knew Chunky didn't play head games. Besides, he'd seen what the block looked like from the other end. They'd tried to make the turn into the block from the other end, only to find their passage blocked by a police van and three patrolmen. As they crossed the intersection, they'd been able to see the center of the block congested with marked and unmarked cars and several ambulances. After they'd crossed, Chunky had dumped his guns beneath the seat and walked back and into the block instructing Total to pick him up at the other end. The block had been on their list of places to go to push back some wigs, that were associated with Ting-a-ling.

"Looks like we jacked this nice Benz for nothing and this motherfucker ain't even got no serious sounds," Chunky said, as he tossed one CD after another into the backseat. "Everybody in the block is kicking it about how Ting-a-ling rolled through the block and capped everything in sight. Three of the four bought the farm, the fourth nigga was screaming your boy's handle while they was shoving him into the ambulance."

"What the fuck happened, this is his shit?" Total wondered aloud as he drove, with no real destination in mind.

"Pressure bust pipes...you got in that nigga's head and he was bonkers and out of there! Oh shit!" Chunky said holding up a CD and checking to make sure it was clean. "This"ll work dog!" he added, then slipped the CD into the player. Biggie Smalls poured through the quad-speakers. *"Where's the stash at... where the cash at...nigga pass that!"*

"Nigga must have really had love for his brother to bug like that," Total said shaking his head in confusion.

"That's a good thang," Chunky said bopping his head to the music as he pulled out his wraparound shades and pushed them on. "Might not have to see that nigga with the police in his ass!"

"Yeah," Total replied, but thought, "*But I need to put him down!*

"But fo' sure, you got dibs on that nigga.... Since the slave ships, with the same clip!" Chunky howled and pumped his fist up and down.

Total just stared at him. It was like Chunky had read his mind, or read the look on his face at the least.

"I'm thinking we shift gears...leave that nigga alone for a few and pay Trench a visit instead. How you feel about that?" Total asked.

"You already know dog!"

❧

Since the car had come from the long-term parking lot out at the airport, they agreed it would be safe to continue rolling in it. An hour later, Chunky let Total again dressed like a derelict out at the scrap yard on 127th and Park Avenue. Five minutes later, Total came around the corner where Chunky was parked. He was pushing a raggedy, canvas mail cart. He motioned for Chunky to follow but hang back. They'd already discussed the specifics.

Ten minutes later, Total stopped in front of what appeared to be just another of the abandoned buildings along the block. Lifting the front of the cart, he drug it up the three steps and into the courtyard. Rolling it against the boarded up entrance to the basement, he pulled out a burlap bag filled with odd pieces of copper and moved to an equally boarded up front door. The door swung open just as he reached for it.

"Get inside!" One of the two shotgun toting men ordered and Total ducked quickly inside.

"What's up?" the second man asked, looking Total over.

"Two grams of that good dope!" Total replied, then stuck two fingers beneath his Navy-styled watch cap and drew out a small stack of folded bills. He let them see it.

"Now this nigger came off!" the shortest of the security guards said.

"Yeh, probably pulled somebody's whole basement out," the other one joked, two on up... second floor, last door to the back!"

"You won't be joking; when your momma calls and tells you she ain't got no water!" the short one laughed as Total went by him and up the stairs. "You'll know where that nigga was all night for sure!"

Total went halfway up the first flight of stairs checking to make sure there wasn't anybody in the immediate area. Sure there wasn't, he set down the burlap bag and opened the mouth wide enough so he could free the two guns it contained. Easing back down the stairs, he peeked around the corner and saw the suppose-to-be guards watching the courtyard through cracks between the double pieces of plywood that covered the door. Their shotguns leaned against the walls next to the door.

Blowing the air out his lungs through his mouth, Total refilled them sucking air through his nose. Feeling calmer, he rushed out and down the stairs. Not taking any chances that either man would get to their shotties, he laced them a good twelve, maybe thirteen times. Catching the nigger that had fell across the doorway by his leg, he drug him out of the way and after a quick peek through the crack, he opened the door and waved for Chunky.

Hoodie pulled low over his eyes, Chunky moved away from the car and strolled up the steps and into the building. As soon as he was inside, he unzipped his long leather coat and pulled out the MP-10 Total had given him.

"We ain't here for no booty...we do this place and raise the fuck up out of here," Total said, clicking the lock on the door. Chunky nodded understanding and they headed up the stairs with Total in the lead.

When Total hit the closed door with his shoulder, the last thing in the world that he expected, was for the door to have just been pushed closed and not even fastened. He tumbled and went down. Chunky ran pass him and deeper into the apartment. Total heard a short stutter from the MP-10 as he was pushing himself up, but then he caught movement out the corner of his eye. Still half-bent over, he fired both guns beneath his body at the three men rushing towards him.

"Bad dope!" Total screamed as loud as he could as he watched one of the trio drop like a bad habit, while the other two peeled off to his right and dove up three steps onto the landing.

"Fo sure dog!" Chunky cried as he came running to the door.

"On the landing! Give them something to think about!"

Chunky stepped part of the way out into the hall and aimed the MP-10 one-handed squeezing the trigger. Plaster and wood went everywhere. Total bent low made a dash for the stairs and saw the two men trying to dig their way into the corner. One of them was pulling a radio from beneath his jacket. Total emptied both guns into them, dropped the clips and was digging for another one, when Chunky ran pass him and tugged at his coat.

"Be out!" he yelled and held up the broken chain with a badge dangling from it, that he'd snatch off the neck of the first man Total had dropped.

"I smelled it!" Total blurted and ran down the steps behind Chunky.

Chunky came out the building, with the HP-10 in one hand and a Glock in the other. Not having time to reload, Total snatched up one of the pump shotguns from against the wall and came out with it ready. There was nobody there and nobody between them and the car. Chunky slid in and across the front seat to the passenger side. Total dumped the shotgun into the backseat and used the key Chunky handed him to start the car and whipped it out of the block.

"What the fuck is going on dog?" Chunky asked still breathing hard, as Total made yet another turn at seventy.

At 110th and Park Avenue, Total slowed the car to a stop and climbed out, with Chunky behind him. They climbed the steps to the subway and as luck would have it, they just had time to buy Metro Cards before the train rolled in.

"Some big time snitching," Total said finally answering the question Chunky had raised twenty blocks back.

"Talk to me dog."

"Come on, the next car's almost empty," Total replied and made his way to the exit door. They took seats at the end of the car.

Total leaned forward and begin telling Chunky what he thought was happening. From the night he'd gotten bagged for slumping Bently Jacobs and his co-defendant at the abandoned building in the Bronx, he felt something wasn't kosher. The police had been waiting for him when he came out. He'd thought then that it had just been a coincidence, but putting together the spot Trench had been bagging up in for twenty years without it ever having been busted, and now cops sitting across the hall from another one of his operations, it all pointed to a setup, and Trench working hand in hand with the police.

Three stops later, they got off the train and flagged down a cab to take them to Bebe's crib. When Bebe let them in, Blaze was sitting up in the living room, his leg up on a stool. A look from Blaze and Bebe made herself scarce.

"Makes sense to me," Blaze said after listening to Total. "But what would really make sense, would be for you both to leave the rest of this shit alone for awhile and think about what you're going to do. You can't go up against the police and Trench!"

"Don't forget Ting-a-ling the ding-a-ling," Chunky threw in.

"I want to Blaze, I swear to God, but I just got this feeling that if I don't handle this now...won't get another chance," Total told him and slouched back against the leather couch's soft cushions.

"You been in touch with Snow?" Blaze asked. "She been hitting my phone like crazy. Said she didn't want to call you and catch you in the middle of something.

"From all sides," Total muttered and dug out his cell phone.

Chapter 30

"You sure baby?" Snow half-whined yearning the loss even before it came.

Before Total answered, he picked up the remote and began doing a channel-check. He stopped on the Channel-4 news. Within minutes, they were showing side-by-side pictures of him, the way he used to look without the dreads and then with the dreads only a bit shorter than they were now. Even with the sound muted, both he and Snow knew that the reporter was informing the viewing audience that he, Jasper Jefferies was wanted not only for escaping, but as "*the*" suspect in a string of murders in and around Harlem. The count was thirteen and three of them had been undercover narcotic detectives. There was a hundred-thousand dollar reward for any information that would lead to his apprehension. "You tell me?" he finally responded.

Pushing Total's head down, Snow switched on

the clippers she had been holding and cut off the first dreadlocks. She shook her head as almost each one fell to the floor. When his head was bald, she picked up the hand mirror and gave it to him. Nodding his head with satisfaction, he set the mirror down.

"Turn this into a goatee," he said stroking the point of his beard. "I think that'll work!"

"How long do you think it'll take?" Snow asked and turned the clippers back on.

"For what?"

"For us to handle whatever and get the fuck out of New York."

"Couple days if we get lucky."

"I hope so," Snow replied and went to work on Total's beard, not voicing her belief that they were due to run out of luck, especially after the last shit at Trench's spot. If Total hadn't fell into the apartment, both he and Chunky would have been inside when the cops rushed it and they'd have never seen it coming.

Snow worked silently for a good fifteen minutes and then gave Total the mirror again as she squatted down in front of him. He looked like neither of the pictures on the tube. In fact, he looked nothing like Jasper Jerfferies at all.

"Smooth as a baby's ass!" Total said smiling as he stroked his jaw. It had been over six years since he'd seen his face. "Gotta try this out," he added dropping his gaze down between Snow's thigh-s and staring hard at the print her pussy lips were making in the tight jeans.

"Yeah, you really should...you know, try it out," Snow said trying not to smile, then stood up and walked her stuff straight at his face.

Whatever Total intended, it was killed as the phone chirped and the disappointment was clear on his face as he stared hard at the offending instrument laying so harmless looking on the arm of the couch.

"Damn!" He muttered and went to pick up the phone. Snow strode out of the living room, heading for the kitchen. She ate when she was frustrated and there was still half of the gallon of cherry-vanilla ice cream she'd started on a couple days before.

"That you dog?" Chunky's voice called through the phone.

"It's me!"

"Don't know how long it's going to last, but we got us a window of sheer opportunity."

"Talk to me Chunky, I need some good news.

It was five minutes before Total got off the phone and went looking for Snow. He found her at the kitchen table, a hand glued to the container of ice cream, as she tried to dig the frozen contents out with a big tablespoon.

"Chunky okay?" she asked, working a wedge free and taking it to her mouth.

"Real good....Listen, how long would it take you to get ready for a party? I mean like, get ready for a party so nobody would recognize you."

"Ten... twenty minutes top. Why, we going to a party?" Snow asked and Total nodded his head yes slowly. "Who invited us?" she asked tossing the spoon over into the sink, the ice cream forgotten.

"You won't believe it."

"Try my chin." Snow got up, closed the container and stuck it back into the freezer, her eyes never leaving his face.

"Ting-a-ling!"

"You're bullshitting!"

"Well he ain't actually inviting us, but he's got a house full of people and according to Chunky they're all blitzed out of their minds."

"We handle it we're out right?" Snow asked.

"Straight out!"

"Gimme ten minutes," she said and ran from the kitchen.

"Nothing like a party to take the mind off your problems," Total mumbled and went to the hall closet for his bag.

Total had just set his bag down near the door, when Snow called him. He went to the bottom of the stairs figuring she was going to tell him she needed some more time and his mouth dropped open at the sight of her.

"Will it work?" Snow asked coming slowly down the steps. Total found himself at a total loss of words. Snow was dressed in a white, body hugging micro-mini dress, matching thigh-high boots and a platinum-blonde wig that caressed her shoulders. White glossy lipstick gave her already full lips a fuller look. Before she hit the bottom step, she put on a pair of white wraparound shades.

"Oh yeah!" Total babbled as Snow came to him and gently pressed her lips to his. "Where in the hell did you get that stuff?" he asked, as she moved pass him and went to the closet to pull down her coat.

"Was saving it...you know, something to add a little spice to things," Snow said over her shoulder as she slipped into the coat.

"That's a lot of spice," Total replied, finding himself whispering unnecessarily.

"You the one that said I dressed too much like a thug," Snow replied smiling widely and began an exaggerated walk towards the door. "You coming?... got a party to get to and people to reach out and touch."

No sooner had Total pulled the car into a parking space, than Chunky showed up beside the car minus his coat. Total hit the lock and he climbed quickly into the car.

"And I thought Buffalo was cold!" he said rubbing his hands together.

"What's it looking like?" Total asked shifting around in the seat so he could look into Chunky's face while they talked.

"Ding-a-ling is there and from what I can tell, he ain't got but three people with him and all of them are fucked up...seriously fucked up like everybody in the house! Dog there's so much shit in there; I had to play the bathroom to suck fresh air to keep from getting a contact and still ain't work!"

"That shit makes you think, so I know you got a plan," Total said, then saw Chunky had shifted his gaze to where Snow sat. "That's Snow dog...Snow!"

"You a lucky dog T," Chunky said shaking his head and turning to look back at Total. "Here's the plan...we go in, find one of 'em and move 'em outside or into one of the empty rooms and put in that work. Hit 'em one at a time and be out!"

"You strapped?" Total asked.

"Stuck my shit in the washing machine...figured somebody might go through all those coats piled in the bedroom."

Reaching down to the floor between him and Snow, Total lifted his bag up onto the seat and unzipped it. Taking out the .38 he'd taken off of Ace Lake, he passed it to Chunky. It was small enough, that with the sweater out like it was, it could be hid in his waistband. For himself, he took out the last silenced 9mm that they bought off Max and slipped it into the harness hidden beneath the hooded Shearling he was wearing.

"Sorry about the party baby, but we need you to stay with the car in case we have to leave sooner than we want to," Total said and bent to plant a kiss on Snow's lip's.

Total hadn't been sure Chunky's plan was based in fact, until he stepped into the house and was engulfed by the rich, pungent smell of Haze. Clouds of it floated up against the ceiling. It took less than three minutes to locate one of Ting-a-ling's crew and with Chunky offering up some 'Dro, Flow had lead the way to the closed door of what turned out to be the den where they could get their smoke on without having to share it. Total popped him, as he dug in his pockets looking for a lighter. They found Chi-low trying to climb into some bitch's womb and did him and the girl stuffing their bodies beneath the huge king sized bed. They hunted for fifteen minutes for Ting-a-ling and the nigga Chunky had said was hanging tight with him, but couldn't find them.

"Think it's time to split," Chunky said after retrieving both his coat and his gun from the washing machine in the kitchen. Total nodded in agreement and they were headed for the door, when Total's phone vibrated. Opening it, he stuck it to his ear and heard Snow scream.

"Yeah smart-assed nigger, that's yo' black bitch... now get the fuck out of my house!"

Total shoved several people out of the way and down as he broke for and out the door. He jumped off the porch without touching one of the eight steps and was running full speed towards the car, before Chunky made it outside.

"Motherfuckerrrrrrr!" Total screamed as he

top of her.

"What now Ting?" Rayshawn asked, straightening up and lighting a smoke.

"We waiting on a call. I couldn't reach Flow or Chi-low, so I called somebody I know can handle this shit!" No sooner were the words out of his mouth, than his phone went off.

"Ting-a-ling, what's up?" Ting-a-ling asked and was about to say something else, when the voice on the other end got his complete attention.

"You might make it from under those bodies son!" the voice told him. "If you ain't playing games and you're holding what you say you're holding."

"I am man, trust me!"

"Then this is what you're going to do. No ifs and or buts and you don't talk to nobody else about this...."

It took four minutes for the voice to give Ting-a-ling his instructions. The nigga had gone over the same grounds three times and then had had the nerve to hang up in his ear.

"That nigga's on my list!" Ting-a-ling growled as he started the truck and peeled away from the curb.

"Who that?" Rayshawn asked from the backseat.

"Don't even worry about it, you'll know soon enough...Right now, you just make sure that bitch's head stays covered up till we get where we going!" Ting-a-ling said snapping at his cousin, only because he couldn't snap on the nigga that had hung the fuck up on him, like he was a nobody-assed motherfucker.

✦

Waiting until the girl was led down the club's basement stairs, Wash and Clay stepped from behind the heavy drapes and into the interior of the club. Wash looked from Trench to Ace Lake's son and some kid he didn't recognize and back at Trench.

"You getting stupider and stupider!" Wash said sticking a finger at Trench's face with each stupider. "Let's go to your office man!" Wash said and headed in the direction, not even bothering to wait for an answer. Clay followed behind him, both of them sneering as the passed Ting-a-ling.

As soon as the three of them were inside the office with the door closed, Trench went off. "Don't you ever call me stupid again! Don't ever disrespect me in front of my people!" he was leaning across his huge desk, his fingertips resting lightly on it.

Clay saw it coming, but besides physically going at his partner, there wasn't a damn thing that he could do to stop it. Wash reached across the desk and grabbed two handfuls of Trench's suit lapels and dragged him across the desk. When Trench's face was an inch or two from his on, Wash stopped pulling. The only thing that remained in contact with the desk that belonged to Trench were his turtle-skin shoes.

"You talking to me, bite-sized nigga? What

you gonna do? Stupid motherfucker! Stupid... stupidddddd!" Wash snarled, his face twisted in anger.

Maintaining his grip on the little man with one hand, he used his other hand to catch Trench's hanging tie and balled it around his fist. "If you ever... try telling me what to do...every toss anything up in the air that sounds like you're threatening me or my partner...I'll bury your pitiful snitching ass!" Wash said, spit flying as he talked.

"I think he's got it," Clay said, trying to play referee.

"Nigga, we out there sitting on your doorstep, trying to keep your petrified ass alive," Wash started up again, as though Clay hadn't even spoken. "And you make a threat? Yeah nigga you pay for it, but remember, you can buy protection...can't buy loyalty or respect!"

"He's good!" Clay shouted as he watched Trench's face turn red, his eyes bulging as Wash raised the tie up into the air forming a noose.

"He better be!" Wash hissed and shoved Trench backwards across the desk and into his huge cushioned desk chair.

"You know how you fucked up right?" Clay asked, walking around to the side of the desk where Trench sat working to loosen the tie. He sat down on the edge of the desk. Trench jumped when he reached out to help him with the tie.'

"I thought I was doing the right thing," Trench blurted. "I figured it was the only way to stop that nigga's bullshit!"

"You ain't paying close attention," Clay said. "You tell us about the girl...we tell you we want to get a look at her without her seeing us...hold!" Clay said raising a hand as Trench opened his mouth to say something. "You pull that off and that's cool, but then you let us walk in your spot and Ace's son and this other nigga that ain't got no business seeing us are sitting there goggling us like we're strippers or something."

"He's the one that took the girl...didn't think," Trench said.

"See Wash! Now we're getting somewhere," Clay said glancing back at his partner, then back to Trench. "You didn't think and because you didn't, after this is over...they belong to you. You get to clean up the mess. Now, getting to the girl. You see the shit this nigga has been doing because Ace, or Ace's kids put her brothers under?"

"Well I heard about it," Trench replied and lit a smoke, his hands still shaking.

"So, what do you think he's going to do with that nigga having actual hands on the bitch?" Clay asked and watched as Trench shrugged his thin shoulders. "Start thinking man...think," Clay added and tapped the side of his head with a finger.

Trench looked back and forth between the two

men, that he had been paying an average of a hundred-thousand each per year for close to fourteen years. The last thing he was supposed to have to worry about, was them flipping on him. But then, everybody had a breaking point. His own had come when they'd stumbled into one of his operations, while hunting for a murder suspect. They'd caught him with his hands directly on two and a half kilos of 97% pure heroin. There had also been over a hundred-grand in cash. They'd confiscated the money, without giving him a receipt--and he hadn't asked for one--and he'd been able to walk away with the satchel of drugs they'd tossed in a dumpster on their way out the building. The payouts had begun small at five-hundred a week, but had grown to include bonuses for advance warnings of impending raids or investigations. The warnings turned out to be the most costly, because they'd also cost him his self-respect. The first time they'd come for a name, he'd folded like a wet Timberland box. They had never asked about drug business, so in his mind he was justified in snitching. They had come once looking for a name to put with a body they'd found in Central Park...the name of the nigga that had left it there. Figuring he could kill two birds with one half-a-brick, he'd sent his people to bump Total off and then called in an anonymous tip to the Bronx authorities. One way or another Total should have been out of his hair.

"We reaching you right?" Wash asked, shaking

Trench from his revelry. Trench shook his head obediently. "That means you'll pay somebody to get rid of our mutual problem before they start running their mouths about us?" Wash asked and Trench nodded again.

"So how do we handle this thing with the girl?" Trench asked putting his cigarette out.

"You let this Ting-a-ling motherfucker contact Total...he don't let on that you involved. He likes to call the shots, you let him do that, only you lead him in the right direction. From what you and everybody else says, this nigga has a fetish about keeping his word...on that I'd rather die than not keep my word shit. Ting-a-ling makes a deal with him to call off the war in return for the girl."

"That takes care of his beef, but what about mine?" Trench asked.

"We, as in Clay and I, pick the place and when he shows up for the girl, they both go down and that ends everybody's beef!"

"Okay...okay I'm feeling that. Every cop in New York is looking for him, you crack his nut, commendation...promotion!" Trench said smiling thoughtfully. "Then we're back to business as normal right?" he said hopefully.

"Almost," Clay replied and stood up.

"Almost?" Trench asked, not trying to look too disappointed.

"We want the money you've got out on him,"

Wash stated, then went on as he stared at Trench. "Any problems?"

Trench would have sighed with relief, if he could have done it and not been seen. Fifty-thousand was nothing. "None Wash, none at all," he replied and stuck out his hand to Clay who was closer. Clay took it. Wash took it afterwards, but not until he'd pulled on his gloves.

"Wait until after we roll and have that nigga call and put it to Total. He'll deal on some sucker shit like that. If that nigga Ting-a-ling get out of hand...remind him that we got a warrant with his name on it for homicide!" Wash instructed and moved over to the door where Clay stood waiting to open it.

Exiting the office, Wash and Clay strode straight pass Ting-a-ling and his people without acknowledging their presence and waited behind the drapes until Trench's bodyguard came to let them out.

Chapter 32

"So why we "*really*" don't want to talk to nephew?" Ben Lake asked, trying to follow his brother's lead.

"What kind of son gives a party with his father laying up dead? It would be a waste of words. Only one thing could make it halfway right and make me willing to listen to what he's got to say!" Al Lake answered.

"What's that?" Ben asked.

"Those cops that went into that club?"

"Yeah?"

"They come out with our nephew in cuffs!"

"Anything else?"

"He's suspect like the rest of those niggers in there and you know how we handle suspect niggers at home.,"

"Let me get this right now Al... they come out with him, we do what us Lake boys do...they come out without him, with us knowing that they're looking for him for murder, we fall in behind him when he comes out and see where it leads us?"

"On him like maggots on a dead rabbit in July, but not for long. He don't lead us to no answers...we snatch him like he did the girl and put those questions to him Ace was talking to us about."

"About hint getting too big for his britches... trying to run things he shouldn't have a hand in?" Ben asked, always liking to be sure about exactly what was happening or going to happen. He was the slowest of the Lake boys, but if you gave it to him clear, he could handle his business along with the best of them and he never had bad feelings about anything he ever did. That was mostly because in couple of days it was gone from his mind.

"You got it right Ben!"

"Then the show's about to start Al," Ben said and motioned with a movement of his head to where the door of the club they'd been watching was opening. He picked up his gun and eased the safety off.

"He's suspect," Al half-whispered not liking to mark one of their own, as he watched both cops come out the club and run across the street to climb into the Navigator truck.

"Ace will turn over in his grave," Ben said and slipped his gun back into the slot in the paneling of the van and slammed it closed.

"Without doubt," Al said and stuffed his own

gun up underneath the dashboard and reclamping it.

"What now?"

"We sit and wait," Al replied and climbed up out of his seat and made his way to the back of the van. "You want something to eat?" he asked, opening the mini-fridge's door.

"Ain't got no appetite right now," Ben answered wearily, his eyes glued to the door of the club. "*Watch for nephew...watch for nephew...watch for nephew*," he began droning on in his head, because he knew that sometimes he forgot shit and this was something he would not allow to slip from his mind.

Chapter 33

"What the fuck you doing Rayshawn?" Ting-a-ling demanded, as he came out the bathroom and found his cousin stroking the inside of Snow's thigh.

"Just fucking with her man!" Rayshawn answered and laughed. "I think she likes it though," he added and walked behind Snow.

"And what the fuck does that mean?"

"If she didn't like it, she'd say something right?"

"Nigga she got duct tape across her mouth!"

"I know, I know!" Rayshawn said bobbing his head and rubbing his hands together.

"Come the fuck on...Lil' nigga wants me to call and have that talk with her nigga," Ting-a-ling said and moved towards the steps leading up out of the basement.

"Get back to you," Rayshawn whispered and made a kissing motion at Snow.

When Rayshawn had joined him, Ting-a-ling led

the way back to the office. Upon knocking, Trench called them in and sent his bodyguard out.

"So, what's the deal?" Ting-a-ling asked, plopping down in one of the two chairs across from Trench.

Trench didn't answer as he watched Rayshawn checking the crystal pieces he had lining one entire shelf in his bookcase, like he was trying to find something a pawnshop would take.

"Sit down Ray!" Ting-a-ling snapped when he saw what was holding Trench's attention.

"Just looking man!" Rayshawn said, sitting down the blown crystal piece of a swan and three small ones connected together. He came over and took a seat tossing one leg up onto the arm of the antique chair.

"You get Total on the phone...fake like the only reason you took Snow was to get him to stop killing motherfuckers long enough to talk. Let him know you want to make a deal," Trench coached.

"The only deal I want is that nigga dead!"

"Just chill young-gun, cause that's exactly what's going to happen," trench said raising one manicured hand. "Snow is the only thing he's going to deal for. You ask for some of the money, some of the drugs he ripped, but in the end you settle for him just giving his word that he'll leave you the fuck alone."

"That's nuts! You can't trust no nut-assed nigga!"

"I've known the nigga since he was in pampers... if he gives his word, it happens. The nigga would rather suck a bullet than go back on his word...trust me!"

Ting-a-ling looked toward his cousin not saying anything and thinking. There was no way in the world he was going to let Total walk, especially after killing his baby brother. On top of that, he was tired of hearing his fucking name, like he was some Murder Incorporated motherfucker. Most of his life, he'd been hearing about the nigga. When motherfuckers were sitting around blowing L's and they started talking about niggas that put in work, Total-E always surfaced. If you wanted a nigga to know you weren't having it, you'd say something like "Fuck me and you're getting Total-E." It's the bullshit and a bunch of hype blown out of proportion. No nigga could be a real dyed in the wool killer and allow his emotions to control him. Expecially emotions for a bitch black enough to pretend she was a manhole cover.

"But the nigga "is" going down?" Ting-a-ling asked, un-pocketing his phone.

"Without double? If he doesn't go down...I'm going down and I intend to be around Harlem a whole lot more years," Trench replied and motioned with a flick of his fingers for Ting-a-ling to make the call.

Chapter 34

"You got to be Daffy Duck, if you go for that shit dog!" Chunky said, from where he stood in the doorway holding bags of food from Speedy's Deli. "Its pure unadulterated bullshit!" there was no calm, no give in his facial expressions.

Total turned, never even have heard Chunky unlock the door and step inside. Total stared in disbelief at Chunky. It wasn't what he had said, but how he had said it. For the first time since they had known each other, every trace of the drawl and the accent that anybody that knew Chunky associated with him had vanished into thin air. Just the way he'd spoken was cause enough to pay him serious attention.

"You heard everything?" Total asked, getting up and coming over to take one of the bags.

"All that mattered and you ain't meeting that nigga nowhere, by your lonesome, unless you're ready to put a bullet in me dog!"

"Chunky..."

"Chunky shit! You think I'm going to let you go out and get yourself slumped...maybe Snow along with you? I pay my debts and I owe babygirl like five-bills over that N.B.A. shit!"

"The nigga's a bitch! He ain't doing shit to me, or Snow. Only reason he wants me to meet him is so he can feel like he bitched me," Total answered.

"Nigga killed Snow's brothers...tried to blank her and then went nuts and spanked niggas handling his work. The nigga will smoke you, if you blink and Snow makes you blink. Trust me dog, I see it in your eyes!"

"I'm telling you Chunky, he just wants to see me look weak," Total said digging through the bag he'd taken and finding one of the pastrami sandwiches he'd sent for. Unwrapping it, he took a bite and looked at Chunky.

"Tell you what then, call Snow's phone...know he's going to answer it. Tell that nigga to cut Snow loose right now...not now, but right now. Then give him your word again, that you'll meet him wherever the fuck he wants you to be and you'll come empty handed. If the nigga is about it, he don't need Snow to get his cookies off seeing you crawl."

Sitting his sandwich down, Total pulled out his phone and opened it, but didn't dial. Chunky mimed punching keys and he dialed. The phone at the other end rang three times before it was picked up.

"This Ting-a-ling?" Total asked, working hard to keep his anger at bay.

"Naw nigga, this Rayshawn...hold!" the voice said then the phone was put down. Total could hear Ting-a-ling's name being screamed, but from way off, then there was the sound of something crashing and one hysterical word was bleated.

"Told you not to leave the bitch alone!" Ting-a-ling's voice said, floating through the phone.

"She's fucking taped up man! What the fuck!" Rayshawn replied, then there was the sound of something being dragged. "Said he wanted you right now! Said it was fucking important, so I come to get you!" he added lying.

"Just shut up...shut up!" Ting-a-ling barked and then any sound from the other end of the phone was killed. Total thought for a second, that the phone had been hung up and then Ting-a-ling was speaking to him. "What's up?"

"Got a better deal for you," Total replied, glancing over to where Chunky sat tearing into one of his sandwiches.

"We already got a deal and it stands, unless you don't ever wannah see your precious Snow alive again," Ting-a-ling told him.

"You should listen," Total said, allowing some of the anger he was feeling to sift through and into his tone on purpose. In his mind, he could see Snow tied to something large and probably thought to be unmovable. He could see Rayshawn leaving the area to get Ting-a-ling and Snow somehow finding a way to move whatever she was tied to, to get as close to the phone as she could to deliver a one-word warning. The remainder of the scenario was irrelevant...them finding she'd moved, dragging her back to where ever and the bullshit, because no matter what was said now was more bullshit. Replaying the muffled sound over and over, made it clear in his subconscious mind that it had been "NO" and it had been Snow.

"Spit it out nigga!" Ting-a-ling shouted.

"You want to live to be an old head right?" Total asked, already knowing the answer.

"You already gave me your word!"

"But I didn't give you my word, I wouldn't call somebody in and hit them to split your wig later did I?"

"I'm listening," Ting-a-ling replied the frustration he was feeling amplified.

"Straight talk...you cut Snow loose right now, from wherever the fuck you've got her and I give you my word, that not only will I show up at the spot you choose...when you say, but that I give you my word that I don't reach out and touch base with nobody about you. Far as I'm concerned, you can live to be a thousand. You understand what I'm saying to you?"

"Naw, explain it."

"All this is about is Snow walking away from

this shit...I want her out the picture. She's out and you decide to cross me, so be it. I done outlived every prediction ever made and I'd rather be dead out in the world, then to live to be a hundred and fifty behind these crackers' walls. I know she's out the loop...I'm good!" Total said, with all the sincerity in his heart.

Once again, the sound on the other end disappeared. Most of it. Total heard Ting-a-ling whisper for Rayshawn to check and see where Trench was at.

"She out of here," Ting-a-ling said returning to the phone. "It's going to take a few, 'cause ain't no need for her to know where she been....Feel me?"

"I feel you, just make sure she's got her phone so I can know it's real and you got my word," Total replied, suddenly finding his mouth and throat dry.

"Phone in hand!" Ting-a-ling said and hung up.

Total turned to a silent Chunky, who had discarded his sandwich and was pulling on his coat. "He's cutting her loose and you heard me give him my word."

"You shouldn't even be talking to me dog!" Chunky said and pulled one of his guns out and checked the magazine. "Not about him!"

"We need to hit the street...maybe roll up around Washington Heights. That's Trench's neighborhood and he's got his hand in this shit," Total said picking up his own coat and pulling it on.

"He's yours...that shit's personal, like mine's!" Chunky said and snatched the hotel room's door open and swept out the room swinging the tails of his long leather coat.

Chapter 35

For fifteen minutes after Blaze got off the phone with Total, Bebe stayed out of his way and remained quiet. It wasn't until he started dressing, that she found it necessary to speak.

"Listen Poppa Bear, you got problems...Bebe got problems," she told him. "The time we've spent together have been the best times of my life and I'm not feeling losing them. It may not ever happen between you and me, but if it does I'm okay with it. I know you feel what I've been feeling, but you're just too old and stubborn to change your ways. Talk to me. Please?" Bebe took one of his hands and held it between hers.

Blaze sighed loudly and glanced down at Bebe. He started to pull away, but he knew what she'd said was as close to being a hundred as it got. Bebe was young and looked younger, but he could still detect the hardness at the corners of her huge green eyes, that had come from digging her way up out of the bullshit that had taken her mother and for a lot of years threatened to take her. She was a lot wiser than she looked and even harder than Blaze believed he was.

"Ting-a-ling snatched Snow," Blaze began, lifting Bebe's hands to his lips and kissing them, as he wondered what he would do if he gave in and later found himself in Total's position. Bebe started to speak, but he cut her off. "He let her go, but Total's going to meet him and he can't do a damn thing if Ting-a-ling wants more than just seeing him bitched up."

"Shit!"

"Total doesn't think it'll come to anymore than a stare-off, but I ain't feeling it. He made me give him my word that I would stay put, in case Snow needed somebody to take care of her," Blaze explained.

"Then he ain't feeling good vibes either! So, what are you getting ready to do?" Bebe asked, pressing herself against Blaze.

"I'm going to crash a party!"

"You gave him your word."

"I look like Total to you?" Blaze asked and Bebe shook her head no. "Ain't him and I ain't lived this long by keeping my word to anybody but my blood... when I give it under normal circumstances. This shit ain't regular!"

Pulling her hands free, Bebe strode back into her

bedroom. She came out two minutes later dressed in cold weather gear and carrying the biggest .45 semi-auto Blaze had ever seen.

"Put it away. I'll go down first and bring the car around to the front of the building," Bebe told him and hit the door.

Blaze stood holding the gun, then dropped the clip and checked to be sure it was fully loaded. Sighing, he checked his watch and headed for the door limping.

Chapter 36

When Ting-a-ling pulled the coat from across Snow's head, she swung her head around wildly trying to figure out where the fuck she was. It took only seconds. The tape that had been around her legs had been taken off so they didn't have to carry her up the basement stairs or out to the truck. She held out her taped wrist.

"When you feel safe...call him and let him know," Ting-a-ling said and un-pocketed a gravity knife. Popping it open, he cut through the duct tape freeing her arms and she reached up and tore the swath from her mouth. Pulling her phone from his other pocket, he gave it to her and then opened the door. Climbing out, he helped her down and then climbed into the front seat with Rayshawn.

A cold chill ran through Snow, as Rayshawn winked at her before pulling off. *"You got it coming!"* Snow thought as she watched the truck turn the corner.

Spinning, she ran to the steps that led up to the overhead subway platform at the corner of 125th and Broadway. She ran up the stairs, stopping just long enough to make sure there was nobody directly behind her and moved to the token booth. A quick search of her coat turned up eighty-five cents in change and they hadn't given her, her shoulder bag.

"Fuck!" she muttered and stepped away from the booth so the woman behind her could buy a Metro Card. Glancing around, she looked for anybody that might be a cop so she could slip under the turnstile, but spotted a "*swiper*" putting people through the last turnstile at a dollar a head. She went to him, but before she could ask him his face widened into a huge grin.

"Snow right?" he asked, even then it was obvious he already knew the answer. "You need to get through?" he asked and then swiped one of the handful of cards he was holding. "You always did me right!"

Snow caught drifts of what he was saying about being sorry to hear about her brothers, but she needed to catch the incoming train and put some space between her and where Ting-a-ling had dropped her, just in case there was a sudden change of heart. She barely made it through the closing doors.

Eying everybody in the car, Snow moved to the door that led out of the car and to the next one. Opening the door and keeping it open with her foot, she dialed Total's number.

"It's me baby!" Snow found herself shouting at the sound of Total's voice on the other end of the phone. "I'm on the Uptown One-Train, it's stopping at 137th Street right now," she told him lowering her voice and watching the faces of anybody that stepped into the car.

"Stay on it baby," Total instructed, "Listen, you know where you can switch over to the A or C-Train right?"

"Yeah," Snow replied as the doors closed and the train started moving.

"Do that. Play the last car and I'll meet you at 110th. Okay?"

"I look like shit," Snow mumble seeing her reflection in the window of the exit door for the first time.

"And you're alive and I still love you...looking like shit and all!" Total said and Snow couldn't help but smile at what she knew was the gospel.

"Me too," Snow whispered and closed the phone.

Chapter 37

"Pray nigga, 'cause if he don't show...your ass is going down and you won't even need a visiting list," Wash snarled and almost took another swing at Ting-a-ling, who was pressed in the corner of Trench's office wiping blood from his split lips with the silk hanky Trench had given him. "Still don't know why you left these niggas here with her!" Wash said turning to face Trench who was seated behind his desk, with his bodyguard standing beside him. His hands were buried deep in his oversized coat pockets.

"Had things to take care of. He brought her to me, how was I supposed to figure he'd cut her loose?" Trench replied, feeling a lot more comfortable in the presence of Wash and Clay with his bodyguard nearby a hand on the gun in his pocket.

"Last shot Trench! They stay here with you until it's time, then you take them there. If he keeps his word, it'll be that much easier," Wash explained as he nervously paced the width of the office.

"He will!" Ting-a-ling blubbered, removing the hanky from his lips and looking at the bloodstain.

"He does...we take care of him and y'all beat a path to somewhere and stay low until we let you know it's okay," Wash replied.

"Where y'all gonna be?" Trench asked standing, but not leaving the proximity of his protection. There was no way he was going to allow himself to be subjected to being smacked around, cop or not.

"You ain't gotta worry about that, just know that if he shows we got him...permanently. Just make sure everybody get's the fuck out of there as soon as the shit starts! Again, if he has the guts to show."

"He'll show!" Ting-a-ling said and glanced to where Rayshawn stood massaging the lump on the left side of his head. Ting-a-ling hadn't prayed to God since he was a kid, but he was praying, that not only would Total show, but that Total would push both of the cops.

"He better for everybody's sake," Wash tossed as he spun and headed toward the door where his partner Clay stood, with a hand of his own stuffed in his pocket. Pulling the door open, Clay let Wash walk out ahead of him and followed closing the door behind him.

They stood at the bolted door until Trench's bodyguard came and let them back out onto the dark street.

"What do you think?" Clay asked as they jogged

across the street to the car.

"He'll show, but you can bet your last dime he ain't coming by his self, or standing there to let no wimp-assed niggas like that crew shove his top-piece back. Word or no word."

"Then what?" Clay asked sliding into the passenger seat.

"We start the ball rolling and clean up whatever's left. No matter what happens tonight, we get rid of Trench, Ting-a-ling and their people!"

"You talked to Spider and his road-dog?"

"They're in...even got somebody to peel Trench's safe," Wash answered and Clay shook his head in agreement and spun his cap around backwards.

"We get pass this...putting in for retirement Wash," Clay said matter-ah-factly, while Wash whipped the car out and into the Downtown traffic.

"You can't do that!" Wash replied, ignoring the car that sped through the red light ahead of them.

"Why not?"

"I'd have to break in a new partner...we got nineteen months till our twenty. You chill and Scout's honor, we can chill and find safe spots to see it out. No more of the cowboy shit!"

"You retiring and leave all this madness to somebody else?" Clay asked and turned so he could look into his boy's face.

"Yeah right! Imagine that!" Wash said and started laughing.

Chapter 38

It was eleven-twenty when the second A-Train pulled into the 110th and Cathedral Parkway station. This time, Chunky remained seated on the old sandbox until he actually saw Snow step off the train. Smiling, he stood up and walked to her with his arms out.

"Scared the shit out of me baby girl!" he said as Snow stepped into his grasp and hugged his waist. "You good?" he asked, taking her by the shoulders and taking a step back so he could do an inventory.

"Ten fingers...ten toes," Snow replied and wiggled her fingers for him. "Where's he at?" she asked looking up along the platform for Total.

"Give you a hint," Chunky said smiling and removing his hand from her shoulder. "He definitely ain't in front of us!" Snow spun around just in time to see Total step from out of the darkened subway tunnel. She ran the half-dozen steps to him and jumped up and into his arms, her arms wrapped around his neck.

"Better let somebody kidnap you at least once a week, if a nigga gonna get served like this," Total said and pressed his lips to hers. "Missed you baby," he whispered as he placed another kiss below her ear as she nuzzled against his neck. He could feel her whole body shaking.

"There's a room upstairs with wheels!" Chunky called, after emitting a short low whistle to get their attention. Two uniformed cops were making their way down the platform stopping to roust the sleepers and nodders.

Setting Snow down, Total took her hand and followed Chunky out through the gated turnstile and up onto 110th Street. They walked a block and made the turn onto Manhattan Avenue to where the van was parked. With Chunky already in the front, Total opened the side door for Snow and slid in beside her.

For a dozen ticks, Snow stared at Total and then with her bottom lip trembling, she asked what was going on as she realized for the first time, that he was once again dressed in his motorcycle leathers.

"You're home, that's all that's going on," Total told her and knew before the words were completely out of his mouth that they didn't even sound right to him.

"Bullshit! You're going to him!" Snow accused.

"I gave my word."

"Fuck your word...nigga's going to murder you! I could see it in his eyes and he's got Trench in his outfield!" Snow replied angrily. "Did you know that?"

"Yeah I know," Total replied and scooped up the helmet that had been laying on the floor.

"You know what? That he's going to try and do you, or that you know he's got Trench in his pocket, which mean they got the police on the team?" Snow asked and then hit him in the shoulder with her balled up fist as hard as she could.

"Both!" Total said absorbing the blow.

"What about your promises to me?"

"I promised we'd leave New York as soon as I handled Ting-a-ling, I promised that I'd take a pass on Trench....! promise you anything else?"

"You're going to go to him and let him kill you, for letting me go?" Snow asked the look on her face twisting Total.

"If he can," Chunky muttered from the front as he snapped a round into the chamber of the gun he was holding.

"Jasper...can't we just leave baby? Just you and me somewhere, where ain't nobody ever heard of you," Snow pleaded her eyes filling with tears.

"It won't work and you of everything alive on this planet, should know I couldn't live like that. Shit would eat me alive!" Total said and tried to reach for her.

"Chunky?" Snow half-cried. Chunky dropped his eyes from where he had been watching them through the rearview mirror. She knew it was useless. Letting her window down, she breathed in the cold air and wiped her eyes on the sleeve of the coat. "Okay...I'm good now," she whispered rolling the window back up. "What do I do?"

"I'm supposed to show up at the Fort in Central Park...Chunky doesn't have an idea where it's at and it's too late in the game to put him up on it. Your job, is to take him somewhere in the park and head him in the right direction. We don't know all the players, so you get him in and get back here. You hang up here until 1:30 or until you hear all hell breaking loose and then you meet us downstairs," Total explained, stroking Snow's hand.

"And if you don't show?" she asked calmly.

"Then you go to Blaze at Bebe's. He'll take care of you." Taking' a quick glance at his watch, Total shoved the door open and got out the van. Snow watched him walk around to the rear of the van and pull the door up. It wasn't until then, that she saw the bike resting on the floor behind her.

"I got him!" Chunky said and climbed out. He walked around to the back and helped Total lift the bike out and down to the ground.

Chunky stared at Total and when Total started to say something, he cut him off. "Everything in that park is yours, but that nigga is mine!"

In silence, Total went back around the van and reopened the door. Picking up his helmet, he reached out and hooked his hand behind Snow's head and pulled her to him. He kissed her hard against the mouth, then spun before she could see what was happening in his eyes.

Snow sat next to Chunky in the front seat of the van until Total's taillight disappeared a half-dozen blocks along Manhattan Avenue.

"Get him back to me Chunky...swear on my momma, I'll owe you my life. He's all I got," Snow whispered and started the van.

Chapter 39

"That's an awful big piece," Clay said, as they moved up the slippery grade towards the Fort. "Know you didn't check that out the armory!"

"It's the motherfucker," wash replied as he slipped and had to allow himself to slide backwards to keep from hitting the ground.

"Try walking in the snow sideways," Clay suggested as he worked his way up the hill to the steps of the Fort. Following his partner's example, Wash made it up and took a seat on the cold steps, cradling the rifle.

"It's an FLN chambered for a .308 round...and this baby..." Wash brushed the snow that was accumulating on the scope off. "This is twelve-power Zeiss night scope, that'll let you quarter one of these damn coons eyes at three-hundred yards without trying," Wash finished and then stood as Clay produced a pair of two-foot long bolt cutters and clamped it onto the lock on the Fort's gate.

With just a little pressure the lock came apart. Removing the pieces,' Clay tossed them down the rocky hill along with the colt-cutters. He swung the gate open and Wash slipped inside. While he waited, he pulled a box containing a new lock and keys from his pocket and got it ready.

"We're set...three hours and counting down," Was said as he watched Clay slip on the new lock. Pulling the wire apart that held the two keys, he gave one to Wash and stuffed the other into the zippered pocket on his camo-vest.

"You still didn't say where it came from," Clay reminded him.

"If I tell you...gotta kill you!" Wash said jokingly and took a running start. He made it all the way to the bottom without busting his ass.

"Whoa!" Clay called as Wash started to walk away and pulled out his vibrating cell phone. "Clay here!" he answered raising the phone to his ear and watching Wash who was making snowballs. Clay listened to the caller for maybe a full minute then tucked the phone away.

"What's up?" Wash asked, standing so Clay couldn't see the huge snowballs he had cupped in his hands.

"You ain't gonna believe this...they're at Ace Lake's house with a warrant and a locksmith. The lieutenant wants us to serve it, if Ace Junior is on the premises. Gotta a delayed concerned sighting after they broadcast Ting-a-ling's picture," Clay explained and pretended to slip as he came down the hill.

"Fuck! Of all the times!" Wash cried and dropped his snowballs to take a look at his watch.

"Oh fucking shit'." Clay exclaimed and Wash turned. The snowball hit him right between the eyes and by the time he could see, Clay was forty-feet away and moving at a jog down the path that would bring him out near the parked SUV.

❧

"Damn!" Clay groaned and spun around and back down the interior steps of Ace Lake's brownstone, almost taking Wash who was behind him down too.

"What's the fuck up?" he asked, his weapon held against his leg as he tracked Clay's progress to the wide open front door with his eyes.

"Bad man...bad," Clay replied shaking his head as he tried to suck up all the cold air there was outside the door.

"Ace?" Wash asked and then began laughing when Clay shook his head yes. "Ain't no room on the force for no soft-assed homicide cops," he joked and went up the stairs two at a time.

Less than thirty seconds passed before Wash came rushing down the stairs, his face looking twisted. He stopped long enough on the porch to instruct the uniforms not to allow anyone into the house but the Medical Examiner. Hopping off the porch, he strode around the near corner--away from their car--and disappeared. Pulling the door closed, Clay followed.

"Well, I'll be a motherfucker!" Clay said at the sight of Wash heaving his guts up against somebody's brand new chrome rims. "I gotta put this in the book," he added pulling out his memo book and flipping through it until he came to a blank page. "You happen to know what today's date is?" Clay asked, as another gusher of vomit poured from his partner's mouth. "Fuck you!" Wash shouted and dry-heaved.

Chapter 40

"This time... we don't lose them," Ben Lake said as he pulled the Dodge Caravan from the curb and fell in behind his nephew's pearl-white Denali. "You see how they had Lil' Ace blocked in?"

"Seen it Ben... means we got to get him loose. Think all those guys is the police?"

"If they ain't it's their bad, cause nephew's coming with us, one way or another!"

"I get the big one. The one with the gun in his pocket," Al declared and opened the compartment on the side of the door and pulled out first one gun and then another.

&

"Almost like home," Al whispered as he trailed his brother through the heavy thickets along the edge of Central Park. Ben glanced up putting a finger to his lips and then made a circling motion. Al nodded his understanding and cocked both of his gun, as he moved to his brother's left so they'd have the entire bunch between them, but without a chance of hitting each other.

Chapter 41

Having stripped off his leather coat so he could move through the brush without waking the dead, Chunky shivered, but continued watching Ting-a-ling and his supporting cast as they made their way up the stone steps. If they kept coming and the Fort was their objective, the natural course of things would bring them right pass him. Closing his eyes and leaning up against the granite boulder behind him, Chunky became all "ears a gun in each hand.

When the crunch of footsteps told him they were within his range, he opened his eyes turned to fire, then held up as he saw two other figures rush from a small gulley a dozen feet away. The sounds of their guns firing, sent everybody to ground, one not of his own volition.

Poised, Chunky waited until he saw the first sign of movement and squeezed the triggers of both guns. Somebody screamed and two of them jumped up and tried to run. From out of nowhere, the roar of a huge caliber weapon ripped through the darkness and one of the runners was picked up and slammed sideways into the brush. Just as Chunky pulled back, a round tore chunks off the boulder he was using as concealment. "What the fuck is that' shit?" Chunky cried aloud, but still ducked down and out and fired towards what he thought was the source until one gun locked back empty. With no hesitation, he rolled backwards and down the small rocky incline he had only recently crawled up.

In the middle of reloading, he heard at least two dozen shot being exchanged and they weren't coming anywhere from the area of the others. This was something new, that needed to be looked into but, first he needed to find out if he'd gotten Ting-a-ling.

Accelerating, Total rode low across the handlebars of the motorcycle and straight at the two men that had appeared out of nowhere and begun shooting at him. The light along the pathway was bright enough, that he knew neither shooter was Ting-a-ling, which meant they were fair game. Steering the bike with one hand, he brought up his gun and went off the road and into the brush.

Shocked at the biker's move, and in danger of being run down Spider and Biggs leaped up to dive out of the way, and found themselves being hammered from behind.

Total saw the gun flashes come from behind the men and just barely held up on firing towards it, as something so big it could only be Blaze came lumbering out.

"Shit getting crazy!" Blaze said, then reached back with his hand to where Bebe was making her way out from between the trees.

"Somebody's up in the Fort with a rifle... a big one! Ain't no way I can make it up there!" Blaze said, his face covered with sweat and pine needles.

"You shouldn't even be here!" Total yelled trying to make sure he could be heard over the racing Suzuki's engine. "Both of you back off...get out of the park and somewhere Snow can reach you if this shit gets any worse," Total added not wanting to come out and say that he feared he might not make it. If the two men Blaze had taken down were in the park and working with either Ting-a-ling, or Trench and the police, there could be a whole lot more "*unexpected*" in the equation.

"We're out!" Blaze said pulling Bebe with him back the way they had come. Whipping the bike around in the slick grass and brush, Total road it back up onto the gravel path he'd been on and headed in the direction of the Fort. Even above the roar of the engine he could hear the bellowing reports of the big gun in the darkness.

Wash had seen Trench, Ting-a-ling and their crew through the scope of the rifle, but because of the barred window of the Fort, he couldn't see anything to his left. At least not until, the two men rushed towards Trench firing. His first shot was reflex and he missed, because he hadn't sighted and saw chunks of earth and snow kick up from the ground. Sighting the second time, he watched one of the two attackers--who had to be with Total. From nearby, he heard Clay's gun barking.

Chapter 42

Fear caught itself all up in Rayshawn's collar as he watched the area around them suddenly light up with the flashes of gunfire from their left. Something slammed into his chest and sent him stumbling nuttily away and to the ground, but he only stayed there for as long as it took him to realize he'd lost his gun. A gun in his hand, he'd stand and wait for a carload of niggas to roll up intending to do a drive by. Without a gun, he knew he wasn't shit. He began crawling back the way they'd come, but sliding down the snow-covered grass hill instead of the stone steps.

◦

Unwilling to be left out, Snow continued to drive around the blocks next to the park, figuring she'd be justified if Chunky suddenly found himself having to bail out and she was close enough to give him a way to get out of the area. It was the only excuse she could come up with, because she had no idea where Total was at.

Snow was just turning onto 110th Street for the second time, when the first gunshots rang out. She slowed the van, trying to keep an eye on the side of the street nearest the park. Before she was halfway down the block, she saw a figure pushup from the ground and start running in a zigzag pattern, holding a dangling arm. When he hit the street, he turned and began waving his good arm at the approaching van.

One second Snow was applying the brakes and with the next she was stomping on the gas and leaning over the steering wheel concentrating. Seeing the van wasn't about to stop, the man tried a few seconds too late to get out of its path. Snow spun the wheel of the van and slammed directly into the man. The impact sent the man flying, only to have him thud against the van's windshield and shatter it.

Braking, Snow jumped out of the van leaving the door swinging and ran around to the front. Rayshawn raised his head, broken and leaking, but alive and that hadn't been the intent. Bringing the .38 semi-automatic Chunky had left with her up from against her thigh, Snow smiled crazily.

"You wanna eat something out?" Snow yelled. "*Eat some of this!*" she said and fired four times into Rayshawn's face and head. Made aware of the presence of a car behind her, by the screeching tires as the driver drove in reverse to put some space between him and what was happening, Snow ran back to the van and jumped in.

Backing up a few feet to swing around Rayshawn's body, Snow put the van into drive and pressured the gas. She felt, but didn't see the back tire thump over the dead body. Halfway through the intersection, Snow decided she was heading in a direction she wasn't familiar with and whipped the steering wheel to the left speeding down Lenox. For a dozen feet after the turn, the van travelled on its two left side wheels before crashing back to all fours.

Snow drove until she hit 113th and then made another left up into the block, knowing it wouldn't be long before someone passed along the description of the van to the cops. She had to disappear and there was only one good place to do that late-night.

Speeding across 7th Avenue, Snow crossed 8th and then Manhattan and drove the ramp down into Morningside Park. Following the asphalt road--her lights out--she pulled the van close up against the bricked park building, where it couldn't be seen from the street. Too close to the building to get out, Snow slid across and out the passenger side. She ran beneath the overhanging trees in the snow, until she reached the foot of the stairs she'd come down to meet Total for the first time.

Creeping up the stairs and staying below the concrete wall, Snow peeked towards Central Park.

There seemed to be two dozen squad cars parked, or racing through the park with their lights flashing. Flipping the gun backwards and into Morningside, Snow stood up and used the shadowed areas to re-cross Manhattan and make her way to the 110th Street subway entrance.

Skipping down the stairs, Snow stared into the startled faces of three crackheads, who'd been smoking by the smell of it. They backed away, letting her pass, but they stood wide-eyed watching her, until she walked down the steps to the next level and sat down. The sound of flicking lighters reached her, but she ignored them concentrating instead on the platform beyond the turnstiles.

Chapter 43

Riding the motorcycle straight up the hill at the rear of the Fort, Total heard the sound of the rifle being fired and came off the bike while it was still moving. The full Bohn body armor that he wore beneath the Alpinestars1 leather gear saved him some scrapes, but he knew he'd be bruised and sore if he saw daybreak.

Coming to his feet, Total moved around the side of the Fort that almost hung over a rocky cliff and sidestepped his way to the front corner. He peeked and found himself within a foot of a rifle barrel protruding from one of the barred windows. Shifting the .357 to his left hand, Total reached out and snatched at the weapon. It moved, but someone was attached to the other end, so he stuck the .357 through the bars and pulled the trigger four quick times. With nothing to stop him, he pulled the rifle free and tossed it down the cliff. He was about to retrace his steps, when the sound of a gun being cocked, froze him in place.

"Don't even think it!" Clay warned as he finished pulling himself one-handedly up from between a rocky niche. Total started to turn his head. "Goodnight nigga!" Clay added and began squeezing the trigger.

The roar of the gun seemed to echo inside Total's helmet, but the impact he'd expected to feel never materialized.

"Naw dog, you say goodnight!" came Chunky's familiar drawl and Total watched him raise up from the ground less than six feet from where Clay lay a huge hole in the side of his head.

"Chunky!"

"Chunky my ass dog, let's get the fuck out of this spot!" Chunky replied running over to where the bike rested, its back tire still spinning. "I don't ride no back seats," Chunky said, righting the motorcycle and straddling it. Total ran over and hopped onto the bike as Chunky accelerated throwing up snow and gravel as the back wheel caught grip.

"Ting-aling?" Total asked, his hands clamped onto Chunky's shoulders.

"Over and out dog! That dressed up pretty nigga made it to a cab before I could reach him!"

"Had to be Trench!" Total blurted, as Chunky took the bike down the stairs both wheels bumping and thumping all the way.

"Take a left!" Total yelled.

"That's the way the cab went!"

"Figures. He's heading for his hole and if we

don't get there before he pulls it in around him, I still got a problem!"

"Always do dog... hold on and let's see if this motherfucker can do that quarter-mile shit in less than ten seconds!"

As Chunky did a hook slide into the one-way street of the block that Total had directed him into, Total pushed himself back and jump off the bike. "Go home Chunky...that's a direct!" Total said, as he watched the taxi turning into the block at the far corner. "It's a wrap here, one way or another."

"Give a nigga a chirp!" Chunky yelled, as he took off down the block straight towards the oncoming cab.

Dropping to the sidewalk, Total rolled over and in between two parked cars. From beneath the car in front of him, he watched the taxi stop. The sound of the door being opened reached him and then he saw feet step down. As soon as the taxi passed him, Total was up and running in a crouch.

Trench was pushing the door to the club open, when Total slammed a shoulder into his ribs. They both crashed into the club and for a few seconds the ripped-down drapes entangled them.

"Nooooo!" Trench screamed as Total raised and brought the weighed butt of the .357 Magnum down against the older man's head, with a sickening crunch.

Stepping back and away from Trench, Total moved to the door and risked a quick glance up and down the block. Seeing nobody visible, he shut the door and bolted it.

Grabbing an unconscious Trench, Total drug him carelessly through the club by his ankles to the office. While Total was trying to find the key to the office from the ring he'd found in Trench's pocket, Trench groaned and Total helped him back into dreamland with the steel toe of his Engineer boot.

Trench was like a Boy Scout and Total found everything he needed either in Trench's office, or on the floor of the club. By the time Trench regained consciousness, Total had him gagged and duct-taped to one of the wing backed Windsor chairs in his office.

"Long time no see," Total said, swinging the goose necked lamp around so the light was in Trench's face. "Don't worry; the tape ain't a problem, 'cause there ain't nothing to be said. You're dead and been dead for like nine years," Total added and leaned back in Trench's huge chair.

"Only question is how a nigga like you goes out," Total went on, as he pulled a K-bar knife from his pocket and opened it in the glow of the lamp. Total pushed himself up and moved slowly around the desk.

Trench actually managed to make the chair he was taped to, jump backwards a few inches as he panicked at Total's approach. Bending beside the chair and then squatting, Total allowed his eyes to roam around the office and finally settle on the massive, squat enameled safe that sat in the corner. Catching Trench's hand, Total separated one finger from the rest and pressed the razor-sharp blade of the K-bar on top of it. One last glance towards the safe and Total raised and brought his gloved fist down onto the flat side of the knife. Trench's thumb came off and he scream-ed into the triple layer of duct tape that covered his mouth.

"As I was saying, ain't no need for you to say nothing," Total said, as he leaned, picked up the thumb and held it close to examine it, before dropping it on Trench's desk. "I can do this all night long...would like it like that, or I can finish it with a pull and leave you so they can leave your coffin open and folks not get sick."

"Paweeze...pweeze!" Trench cried through the tape as huge tears ran down his face and beneath the edge of the tape.

"No talking...no begging, just a simple deal," Total said standing and moving around to the other side of the chair. Trench clamped his hand closed. "Way I see it, you've got five fingers left on this hand...show me with those fingers, how I'm going to get inside your safe." Pulling the .357 from his waistband, Total layed it on one side of the thumb. He placed the knife on the far side so they framed the leaky digit. "You make one mistake and the deal's off! That means I'll have to figure out what I can and can't cut off to keep you alive at" least until morning."

Hopping up on the edge of the desk, Total stared uncaringly into Trench's eyes. "Talk to me...oops, my bad," Total said raising his hands up to his shoulders as though he had really forgotten Trench couldn't answer him. "Show me...now!" he finished and let a small smile play across his lips.

Trembling from his reptile-encased feet to his head, eyes bulging, Trench opened his hand and showed five finger. Reclosing it, he showed three more fingers.

"I think that's an eight right?" Total asked and Trench shook his head. Total moved to the safe, spun the dial to clear it and then dialed up the eight.

It took less than three minutes for Trench to relay the right combination to open the safe. Upon seeing the contents, Total took a step backwards and squatted. Total had seen a whole lot of money in his years, but nothing--all at once--that compared to what he was seeing. Reach inside, he pulled out three banded stacks of money and noted the amounts that had been written in ink across them.

"Twenty-five   thousand...twenty-thousand... twenty-thousand," he muttered dropping the stacks to the floor. "Looks like you bought yourself a funeral nobody in Harlem is going to forget," Total stated and then stood and went to the wall where a crumpled duffle bag rested. Tossing it over beside the safe, he dug into the pocket of his leather jacket and pulled out a long wire. Wrapping one end around his gloved hand, he did the same with the other and moved behind Trench's seat.

"Ouupahmus...pahmus!" Trench cried as the wire snaked down over his head.

"Don't think I did," Total whispered as he bent close to Trench's ear. "Positive of that...think I said something about finishing it with a pull," Total added and began pulling the wire he'd taken from the club's piano tight.

Chapter 44

Waiting until the C-Train pulled out of the empty station at 116th Street, Total jumped down off the platform and onto the tracks. Pulling the heavy duffle bag down onto his shoulder, he entered the tunnel. Ten feet inside the darkness, he found the ladder bolted to the side of a two-foot ledge and shoved the bag off his shoulder and up onto it. Climbing up, he caught one of the handholds and began walking dragging the bag behind him. The duffle bag was so heavy, he'd been forced to sit it down and rest every-other block until he'd happened across a discarded C-Town shopping cart. With less than eight blocks to travel, the cold had finally gotten to him enough that he'd drug the bag down into the station. The station had been cold too, but just being inside out of a thirty-mile an hour wind rejuvenated him enough to finish his trek.

Stopping just short of the light that filtered into the tunnel and up onto the walkway he'd been travelling, Total took in the platform and as expected, it was empty, but it was too empty. Snow should have been there. It was after five in the morning, but he'd convinced himself that no matter how long it took for him to get there, that she would wait. She hadn't shown up at Bebe's, where her and Blaze had been waiting and when he'd tried to call her phone, it had rang and continued to do so until he had been forced to cut it. A quick call to Chunky allowed him to learn, that he was at the airport chasing shorties while waiting for his flight back to Buffalo.

Dragging the bag behind him, Total walked out onto the platform and immediately stopped as the sound of a female giggling caught his attention. On the Uptown side of the tracks, a crackhead was holding a crackstem high above the head of the girl he was with and forcing her to jump in her attempts to capture it. She giggled with each failed attempt. Their actions alone were enough to assure Total that there weren't any police in the station. Moving off, a worried look began etching itself onto Total's face.

Halfway along the platform, the clicking sound that always came from the tracks before a train actually pulled into the station, made Total stop and take a look to check the train's distance. It wasn't in sight, but he knew it was on the way.

"Shit," he muttered and then turned as he heard feet coming down the stairs that led out onto 110th Street. Leaving the bag where it was, Total moved to the barred gateway and looked up the stairs. He could see feet and legs, but nothing more until two niggas came running down the steps. One of them swiped a Metro Card and they both pushed into and through the caged turnstile at the same time. They were less than a dozen feet from where he stood and it took only an instant for him to recognize the coat one of them was holding, as he checked the huge pockets. It was Snow's.

Unzipping his jacket, Total started towards them. The only thing that saved their miserable lives was what the one going through the pockets said, as he leaned out from the platform to check for the train.

"Come on train...for that bitch wakes up!"

Retracing his footsteps to the duffle bag, Total lifted up onto his shoulder with the help of his knee and moved to the exit, the two men had come through. Jamming the bag against the bars, he shoved through. Pulled between the incoming train and the need to know, Total climbed the steps. Halfway up, he dropped the bag and moved towards the figure curled up against the wall sound asleep. There was no mistaking the boots or the outfit, it was Snow.

"Come on sleepyhead," Total whispered his lips brushing and en-haling the scent of Fendi. He kissed her ear and Snow turned to look at him as she rubbed her reddened eyes.

For several seconds, Snow stared at Total as though what she was seeing was something totally alien. "Total?" she asked thru dry lips.

"Yeah, but you really look like shit!" Total replied and laughed with relief. Snow snaked her arms around his neck and pulled his lips down onto hers. They were in full lip-lock mode, when two heavy coated uniformed police came running down the stairs.

"Get the bag off the stairs and find a hotel!" one of the cops yelled back as they went pass them.

"Its good baby," Snow whispered urgently as she continued to hold onto Total's wrist to keep him from pulling the gun from beneath his jacket.

"Whoa!" Total said relaxing and standing up. "Let's get the hell out this station...suddenly it ain't all that friendly," he said running down the steps to retrieve the bag.

Almost eighteen years later and they were still the odd couple, as they trudged up the partially snow-covered hill, the duffle swinging between them, with Total dressed in dirty, tattered leathers and Snow in a micro-mini and thigh-high boots that would have been more at home on a whore stroll, or in the fantasies of a long-denied convict. They moved up the hill, stopping from time to time to hold hands and kiss. The undercover cop sitting at the circle, at the top of Morningside Park never associated them with the van he was watching, or the massacre in Central Park.

NEW VISION
PUBLICATION

P.O. Box 2815
Stockbridge, GA 30281

Or

P.O. Box 310367
Jamaica, NY 11431

Order Form

Name: _____

Address: _____

City: _____ State: _____ Zip: _____

Qty.	Title	Price	Total
____	Tit 4 Tat 1	$15.00	____
____	Tit 4 Tat 2	$15.00	____
____	Tit 4 Tat 3	$15.00	____
____	Damaged	$15.00	____
____	Still Damaged	$15.00	____
____	A Blind Shot *(special)*	$8.00	____
____	Boss Lady	$15.00	____
____	Shank	$15.00	____
____	Unfaithful To The Game	$15.00	____
____	The Price of Loyalty	$15.00	____
____	Thicker Than Blood	$15.00	____

Subtotal: _____
Shipping fees: _____
Total: _____

Books will be shipped within 7 business days once payment has been processed. All shipments will go out media mail. First book ($3.85); each additional book is $1.50 per book. No personal checks will be accepted. Make institutional checks or money orders payable to: **New Vision Publication** or go to **www.NewvVisionPublication.com** to place an order.

NEW VISION
P U B L I C A T I O N

P.O. Box 2815
Stockbridge, GA 30281

Or

P.O. Box 310367
Jamaica, NY 11431

Order Form

Name: _____

Address: _____

City: _____ State: _____ Zip: _____

Qty.	Title	Price	Total
_____	Tit 4 Tat 1	$15.00	_____
_____	Tit 4 Tat 2	$15.00	_____
_____	Tit 4 Tat 3	$15.00	_____
_____	Damaged	$15.00	_____
_____	Still Damaged	$15.00	_____
_____	A Blind Shot *(special)*	$8.00	_____
_____	Boss Lady	$15.00	_____
_____	Shank	$15.00	_____
_____	Unfaithful To The Game	$15.00	_____
_____	The Price of Loyalty	$15.00	_____
_____	Thicker Than Blood	$15.00	_____

Subtotal: _____

Shipping fees: _____

Total: _____

Books will be shipped within 7 business days once payment has been processed. All shipments will go out media mail. First book ($3.85); each additional book is $1.50 per book. No personal checks will be accepted. Make institutional checks or money orders payable to: **New Vision Publication** or go to **www.NewvVisionPublication.com** to place an order.